JERRY SWIFT AND CHIRON'S PRIDE

by

Nick Korolev

Book 1

The Jerry Swift Series

Jerry Swift and Chiron's Pride

The author has approved the final PDF of this book.

Crossroads Publishing, LLC – 620-204-1710

www.crossroadspublishingllc.com

ISBN: 978-1-970396-12-6

Edited by Leah Pugh

Cover Illustration by Nick Korolev

Cover Layout by Tonya Andrews

Reality is not only stranger than we conceive
but stranger than we *can* conceive.
J. B. S. Haldane, Biologist

Toto, I've a feeling we're not in Kansas anymore.
- Dorothy, *The Wizard of Oz*

Table of Contents

1

The Stone and the Brain-Dead Jock

Oh, if you haven't heard, I'm a horse's ass.

At least according to that brain-dead senior jock, Andrew Collins, our once illustrious quarterback for the Greenville High School Stallions. And he's the cause of this whole mess. Along with the fact that magic is real, and not just part of the *Dungeons and Dragons* games, a couple of my best friends and I are addicted to at present.

If you don't believe in magic, as in the world of Merlin or Circe and so on, you might as well just stop reading and go play a video game. I learned the hard way. There is a whole hidden and very dangerous world out there, especially when space-time dimensions collide. But there is more that is good, and it took me a while to discover.

My name is Gerald Swift. I'm a junior at Greenville High School and hate about every minute I'm there. See, I'm a genius and take several special gifted classes. No, I'm not bragging. My few friends are also intellectually gifted, and we are referred to as "the geek squad" by the Neanderthals that don't value intelligence or are afraid or just plain jealous of us.

Unfortunately, that includes a few teachers; particularly the gym teacher, Jim Thornton, who is also the football coach. It is a hard truth, but we have to live with it. I try to cut them some slack, but Greenville is in horse country right outside of Lexington, Kentucky where there are an awful lot of rednecks with an attitude against anyone different than them. Especially in the intelligence area. They all think they can take their teenage or adult angst out on us and usually do.

Some people either can't or won't understand that just because their lives are a mess, it does not give them the right to mess up someone else's life just because that particular someone is different than them. I know, I'm venting, but it is an aspect of my life that must be told before I drag you too deep into my world.

My closest friends and fellow IQ geeks, Ben Clark and Alice Gibbons, feel the same as I do and our only solace is our weekly games of *Dungeons and Dragons* with my aunt Bonnie on the farm next to ours.

It is not a video game.

It is the original boxed kind of game from the 1980s with maps, blueprints, character charts, small painted metal figures, special dice, and run by a Dungeon Master who is the referee. It takes imagination and teamwork, things so lacking for us in the school environment more often than I like to think about and, of course, single shooter video games.

My Aunt Bonnie is the best Dungeon Master I've ever known. She grew up playing the game and continued with it in college. She is my father's older sister by two years, tall and willowy, with brown hair just starting to go gray and has expressive brown eyes. Some of the locals think she is quite eccentric.

She is a widow, a published author of best-selling cozy mysteries, raises fancy chickens in one part of her barn, and has turned the other part of her barn into a small horse boarding facility with eight box stalls, a small office, two fenced in arenas, and a nice pasture. One of the stalls is occupied by my sister Ann's prize sorrel thoroughbred show jumper, Gold Coast. Aunt Bonnie's whole place sits on forty acres. It's mostly pasture with a small apple orchard next to a stand of thirty-five acres of woods owned by a nonresident that abuts my parents' farm of sixty acres presently all in corn with my mom's vegetable plot in a corner by the house.

Things started going bad in my life at the end of April, just before final exams set for the middle of May. My friends and I were all at Aunt Bonnie's house Wednesday evening finishing up a game at her big dining room table with all our gaming stuff spread out. Aunt Bonnie was behind her Dungeon Masters screen ready for the last game turn of the night.

Ben was playing a dwarf named Fredrick, which was kind of a funny character choice with him being a tall wiry kid, brown as mocha who would make a perfect Olympic runner. Alice had an elf warrior princess named Golden Hawk which almost fit her perfectly, her having long, kinky blonde hair, but was not quite as thin as her character being built more like a Viking warrior princess. I was playing a wizard named Aden since I'm more into magic than brute strength in dealing with problems in a fantasy world. All of us were in a dungeon room about to be attacked by an unknown enemy on the other side of a thick oak door.

I announced, "We are ready for combat. I have a fear spell ready. Frederick will force the door."

"I'll guard the rear with my rapid-fire crossbow," Alice declared.

"Okay. The party is set," Aunt Bonnie said and rolled the dice to see if Frederick forced the door. "It opens. You see a half a dozen goblins."

"Let me at them!" Ben had Frederick say.

"You can't be surprised by them, but they can be surprised by you." Aunt Bonnie rolled for surprise. "No. Roll for initiative, please."

"I got a two for Frederick," Ben said with disappointment in his dark eyes.

"Let me roll. . ." Aunt Bonnie rolled her dice. "The goblins have the initiative. They must have heard you, Frederick. They charge yelling, 'Kill the dwarf! Chop them all to hamburger!'"

We all started rolling our dice to resolve the combat, do morale and damage checks. The goblins fought until they were all dead and none of our party took serious damage.

"Well, it's ten o'clock and you guys have school tomorrow. We'll start next Wednesday with a wandering monster check where we left off tonight," Aunt Bonnie publicized and folded her Dungeon Master's screen.

The full moon was bright and directly overhead when we left her house, congratulating ourselves on our victory and discussing what we might meet in the next round. Ben and Alice stopped to wait at the driveway entrance as Alice took out her iPhone to call her mom to pick them up, and I started my short walk home. As I turned to say good-bye, I noticed something small glowing on the side of the road where the blacktop met the grass.

"Hey, look." I went over to check.

It looked like a small, glossy, polished stone similar to one you might find in a stream or on the beach and was about the size of a half dollar. I picked it up. It felt as smooth as glass and I thought it might be moonstone, but it glowed a bluish green like foxfire.

Ben and Alice came over for a peek.

"Cool," Ben said. "Perfect for your wizard costume at the next Comic-Con we go to."

"Wonder what it is and who lost it," Alice commented.

A black Ford F-250 pickup truck came roaring down the road at a fast clip and slowed as it reached us. The truck belonged to Ed Foster, the fullback of the Greenville Stallions. In the bed were four more of the team and one of them was Andrew Collins. He had been in a bad mood all week because his truck was in the shop with a burned-out transmission, which was his own fault, by the way. We won't go into it now.

"Shit," Ben muttered under his breath.

Ed slowed the truck to a stop. We all knew their favorite hobby was "geek baiting" as they called it. Andrew jumped out of the truck bed and strode over to us like an Orc about to start a fight. He was big and bulky like one, too.

"Well, if it isn't the geek squad. On your way home from the game with your auntie and the tiny dolls? Huh, Swift?" he sneered. His sycophantic friends laughed like it was the greatest joke in the world.

I closed my hand over the glowing stone, but not fast enough. He noticed it.

"What's in your hand, nerd?" he demanded, closing the distance between us.

"Why don't you mind your own business?" Alice snapped from behind him.

He instantly turned on her. "Why don't you? Or are you thirsty for a hooking up? We can arrange that."

His friends snickered lasciviously.

My anger exploded at that point. "Don't you talk to her like that!"

My hand with the stone in it was raised before I noticed I did it. Andrew was on me in a flash. He grabbed my wrist in a vise-like grip that, I swear, stopped the blood flow while his other hand tore the glowing stone from my fingers, practically breaking them.

"You gonna hit me with your magic pebble?" He held the glowing stone over his head well beyond my reach. "You are such a horse's ass, Swift. A real horse's ass!"

He shoved me backwards as if I was nothing more than a tackling dummy. I landed so hard on my butt in the weeds on the side of the road that I bit my tongue. He looked at the glowing stone, spit on it and threw it hard all the way into my parent's corn field about thirty yards away. He turned on me, balling his hands into fists.

In that second, we were all illuminated by the high beams of Alice's mom's Toyota. A horn blared. Andrew frowned, scrambled back into the truck bed, and it sped off, kicking loose dirt and gravel all over us, the occupants all howling and laughing.

Ben helped me to my feet as Mrs. Gibbons stopped the car, leaned over, and opened the passenger door from the driver's seat.

"What's going on? Is everyone okay, Jerry?" she asked.

"I'm okay. The Neanderthals were messing with us like always. Bad timing." I had the coppery taste of blood in my mouth.

She frowned as Ben and Alice got into the car. "It looked like it was about to get violent. They should be reported. In fact, I think I'll be making a call to Principal Archer in the morning. This bullying has gone far enough."

"It won't do any good," Alice said miserably. "They are jocks that won the state championship this year. They're all heroes and untouchable."

"We'll see about that," Mrs. Gibbons said.

And that was the start.

The next day in school, it all got worse–a lot worse. The morning gifted class in math followed by world history and music were fine. It was lunch where the first subtle hint of colliding worlds made itself known. I was in the lunch line and oblivious to what I was doing, as the confrontation with Andrew replayed itself in my mind for about the millionth time. When I reached the checkout to do my thumbprint on the computer pad to charge it all to my lunch account, I heard Alice's voice behind me.

"You have enough for three people on your tray." She laughed.

I looked down as I put my thumb on the computer pad and found she was right. I could hardly see the tray for all I had piled on it: a mountain of salad, three pieces of pepperoni pizza, about twenty chicken nuggets, at least a quart of mashed potatoes, two bananas, and three oranges.

I shrugged. "I'm just hungry, I guess."

Ben passed by and cracked, "Hungry as a war horse? Man, that's more than I ever saw you eat."

I laughed and started to follow him to a corner table the three of us usually shared when Andrea Baker, Andrew's "Bae", a dark-eyed knock out, oblivious to my presence darted in front of me from talking with one of her very fashion-conscious girlfriends with pink hair at the next table. I ended up stopping short; the load of food on my tray shifted to a perfect example of Newton's Laws of Motion and went flying all over her. She screamed as if she were attacked by a giant spider. Teachers on lunch duty came running, as did Andrew.

"It was an accident! She jumped in front of me and I stopped short," I said to the first one who reached me, Mrs. Downs the math teacher.

"You did it on purpose!" Andrea yammered, brushing salad off her shoulder and mashed potatoes out of her hair.

"I doubt that very much. I witnessed the whole incident. You need to watch where you are going," Mrs. Downs countered, getting a black look from Andrea.

Mr. Thornton was blocking Andrew from coming closer. With a vein pulsing in his neck, and muscles tight, Andrew looked ready to kill. Principal Archer was on his way into the cafeteria, spotted the gathering crowd, and headed over, frowning.

Andrew's face twisted in a savage scowl. He blurted out, "You're not only a horse's ass, you eat like a horse and are clumsy as one!"

As much as I wanted to come back at him with some clever retort, I stayed silent as Principal Archer arrived. "Shut up, Collins. Go finish your lunch. And that goes for you, too, Swift."

"It was an accident," I added and got the hairy eyeball from Archer, Thornton, and the Neanderthal Andrew Collins.

"Mr. Swift happens to be right," Mrs. Downs added. "Miss Baker was not watching where she was going and cut right in front of him."

Well, at least a fight was avoided and things calmed down for a moment, thanks to Mrs. Downs. Principal Archer dropped the issue. The custodian came to clean up the mess. The police officer assigned to be a roving security guard at the high school came into the cafeteria to keep the peace.

I filled my tray just as full again and added three cartons of chocolate milk under questioning glances from Ben and Alice. We all ate in silence, getting black looks thrown at us from Andrew, his football Neanderthals, dear Andrea, and her minions at the table across the aisle.

And yes, I ate everything on my tray, suddenly ravenous and totally oblivious to what was happening to me on a different level thanks to Andrew's big mouth on Wednesday night under a full moon. But I'd find out about how powerful those words were not much later.

2
Four Legs Are Better Then Two

Not having a car, which in a way was a good thing, I took the bus home with my sister, Ann. The only homework I had was to finish my college level calculus. That didn't take long, and I was ravenous for dinner. Mom had made her famous mac and cheese and burger recipe in her crockpot to be ready in case she got tied up at her real estate office.

It was usually enough for her to use as a side dish the next night, but I ate three helpings while talking to the family about the disaster of the lunch at school. I got a few strange looks from everyone, but it all ended without further questions. iPhone use was not allowed at the dinner table, so Ann and I always let our parents know how our day went as part of the dinner conversation. It was her turn.

At least Ann, all blue eyes and cute in a pixie sort of way, had had a normal day in ninth grade and was presently fascinated with the exchange student from England. A kid named Robert Dickerson attended some of her classes. Well, more like a teenage crush, if the truth be known. She talked about him all the time and it always about bored me to tears.

"Robby was at my table for lunch today," she announced, avoiding eye contact with everyone as she stuffed a fork of mac and burger into her mouth.

"And how do you feel about this Robert Dickerson, besides loving his English accent?" Dad asked with a devilish smile. He taught physics at the University of Kentucky and looked like Clark Kent when he wore his glasses.

"Robby's okay. I found out today he even likes horses and has ridden to the hounds . . . you know . . . fox hunting. But I have to concentrate on getting ready for that big stadium jumping event in June, the Cross-County Hunter Jumper Horse Show. It's at the Kentucky Horse Park Rolex Stadium this year. Big money prizes with first place in each division getting $10,000 and championship points. Not about to miss that.

"It could eventually get me and Gold Coast into the U.S. Equestrian Team and future Olympics if we win big, and that would be a dream come true. Robby said he may come to watch since he is spending the summer here before he returns to England," she rattled on and grinned, putting Mom at ease.

Mom looked like a younger version of Professor McGonagall in the *Harry Potter* movies and had a personality to match. She was a horse show mom instead of a soccer mom. Still, you didn't want to get on her wrong side.

Our parents always worried more about Ann in the teens crush area. I was a geek and those of us with a higher intelligence didn't get sucked into romance so easily. Probably because we think deeper about everything rather than let emotions take over. Of course, that led to more worrying from over analyzing things. Besides, Mom had told us long ago no boyfriend, girlfriend stuff before seventeen. We had to enjoy being kids first. How she came up with that age, I have no idea.

I spent most of the night upstairs in my bedroom on Facebook instant messaging with Ben and Alice in a not so hot debate about rolling up more characters for our *D & D* adventures rather than dealing with NPC characters Aunt Bonnie created by rolling dice and. she controlled to add numbers to our group of adventurers. That is, if she would let us run two characters each.

We had our reasons to suggest the idea. NPCs were often not trustworthy or had the misfortune of being temporarily charmed, confused, or deluded, which often put the party in danger. I knew we could roll up far better extra characters we could add to our party and under our control all the time. We all agreed that it would make for a more challenging game.

After placing my iPhone on the charger, showering and pulling on an over-sized *Star Wars* t-shirt, I got in bed and read the last chapter of the *Harry Potter* book, *Order of the Phoenix*. I started the series at the beginning of the week and must admit over the last few years, I had been sidetracked by a ton of other science fiction and fantasy books when not involved in gaming. Though I knew the premise and popularity of the series and had seen all the movies, I still wanted to read the books. Books are always better than movies, in my opinion.

I went to sleep fast and started to have really strange dreams. Not nightmares, mind you. They were just really crazy stuff that only a psychiatrist could analyze. I was in the middle of one dream of the Forbidden Forest with centaurs carrying off Coach Jim Thornton instead of Professor Umbridge when my whole world literally crashed. My bed collapsed under me and woke me up with a bone shaking jolt.

The reason became abundantly clear in seconds. I was instantly shocked when I glanced toward the foot of my bed in the pale moonlight filtering through my bedroom window curtains. There was more of me on the flattened bed.

My whole upper body down to the hips was attached to a body of a horse lying on its side with legs draped awkwardly over the mattress sides half covered by my quilt. I was a centaur!

I went to scream in terror but thrust both hands over my mouth to stop it. My first thought; *was anyone going to investigate the crash?* I had to have made enough noise to wake the dead! There was no place to hide. It was a struggle to get up on my feet.

Hooves thumped on wood floors and skidded on the quilt and a throw rug. Once up and standing awkwardly with my legs spread for better balance, I froze, listening. Nothing stirred. I felt a little lucky my family members were all heavy sleepers, but that was as far as feeling lucky went. There was no way in hell I could stay. My family would be mortified, if not scared to death.

I took a deep breath—had to think logically. I had an old farmhouse staircase between me and my escape through the front or back door. I had to weigh nearly half a ton. Would the stairs take that kind of weight? Well, I remembered the big burly moving men taking my parents' antique oak bed up the stairs when we moved in. All together they had to be close to my present weight. So, I decided to risk the attempt. I had no choice.

I got my legs properly under me and walked as quietly as possible to my bedroom door. It felt strange to be taller. Moving four legs was awkward at first. I opened the door a crack. No one was in the hall. Both the hall and the stairs had carpet, so that would help to muffle sounds and keep me from slipping on the stairs.

A nightlight glowing dully from near the bathroom at the end of the hall provided all the light I needed to see. I opened my door and stepped out into the hall with my right front hoof. A board creaked. I froze. All was dead silent.

Slowly, I walked out of my bedroom with just inches to spare on each side, happy I now had good control of all four feet. The hall floorboards creaked with each step and had an effect on my nerves of fingernails being scratched down on a blackboard.

When I arrived at the top of the stairs, I made the mistake of looking down. The steepness made me dizzy for the first time in my life. There was no way I could go down the front end first, so I decided to back down and hang on to the banister to keep steady.

"Jerry, is that you?" Ann's sleepy voice suddenly sounded from near her door.

My heart about jumped into my throat. "Sh-h-h! Who else would it be? Go back to bed."

"What was all that noise?"

"I had a nightmare, rolled out of bed, and knocked over my night table. I'm fine. Go back to bed, or you'll wake everyone. I gotta pee." I quickly swung myself around to point my butt at the stairs and bumped my hip against the wall in the process.

"Night," she drawled sleepily, thankfully ignoring the thump.

I froze, listening again. Nothing moved in her room or my parents' room on the opposite end of the hall. Satisfied, I began slowly backing down the stairs one set of legs at a time, gripping the banister for better balance. The stairs creaked in protest, but I made it to the bottom. Then, it was on to the living room and the front door. I stopped short at the foyer. The floor there was covered in black and white marble tiles dating to the 1920s. They would be as slippery as ice. I never gave it a thought before, but didn't fancy a fall this late in my escape.

I turned around and headed toward the big country kitchen. The floor there was covered in vinyl with a textured imitation wood board pattern, but it was not nearly as slippery. However, Oscar, our huge domestic short-haired tiger cat was there munching his food and about had a fit at the sight of me coming into the kitchen. He howled and bolted for the living room right between my legs, knocking his water dish over.

In my effort to avoid stepping on him, I stumbled and staggered in a wild dance, slipped on the water, crushed the kitchen table against the kitchen island with my butt and broke my fall by grabbing the kitchen counter. I heard my parents' feet and voices upstairs and Ann yell. I was out the back door as quickly as I could get my feet under me, leaped off the porch, galloped around the back and side of the house and down the gravel driveway to the road to stop on the other side of the huge oak on our property.

Every exterior security light went on around the house. I saw Dad appear briefly around the corner of the house by the top of the driveway with a shotgun in hand and look towards me. I was in the pitch dark with the oak in front of me for extra cover.

If he did glimpse anything, he would think he saw a horse and that would confuse things. When he disappeared around the back of the house, so did my hope of ever seeing my family again.

I had to figure out this mess. I could only think of one person who might be of help: Aunt Bonnie. She was quirky, open-minded, and understood stuff most other people of a more conservative mind set didn't.

I decided to go over to her house and hide in her barn for the rest of the night. I'd see her in the morning when she came to feed her chickens and boarders and hoped she would not freak out at the sight of me.

3

A Horse is a Horse and I'm Not

I galloped down the side of the road past our cornfield to Aunt Bonnie's farm. Thankfully, no cars were on the road at that late time of night. The only light on at her place was the security light by the barn. There was a lock on the door, but I knew where she kept an extra key hidden behind the small loose third stone down in the foundation on the corner by the water pump. I retrieved it easily and gained access, closing the barn door behind me.

The seven horses there immediately woke up and started nickering.

"Oh, shut up. I'm not one of you," I snapped irritably. I was in no mood to wake Aunt Bonnie and have her call the police, thinking someone was up to stealing horses or something else of value.

After putting the key on the office window ledge, I made my way down the aisle to the only empty box stall on the right. I discovered I could see quite well in the dark. The stall had fresh clean sawdust bedding ready for a new boarder. It would do for the night. I went in, closed the stall door behind me, and lay in the bedding feeling miserable.

My whole normal life had been snatched away and now, having time to think about it, I didn't know why or how. My mind was in too much shock to think logically. I just lay there listening to the night sounds, horses thumping around in their stalls, heavy breathing and snoring, mice scuttling in the walls, and spring peepers outside.

There was the siren of a police car speeding past to my house. I could only imagine the panic everyone would be in over my disappearance and the wrecked kitchen. I wondered if the siren would wake Aunt Bonnie. Real sleep would not come for me.

Still, I must have dozed off because the clattering of the barn door sliding open, Aunt Bonnie talking to herself, and the overhead fluorescent lights flickering on awakened me with a start. It was about 5 a.m. I saw it on my wristwatch. I hadn't taken it off when I turned in earlier in my real bed.

"What is going on? This is not right. Did I forget to lock up last night? Why is the key on the office window ledge? There's just been too much upset. Ann, you here?" Aunt Bonnie rattled on.

Through the spaces between my stall door boards, I saw her come in and pick up a bucket sitting on a bale of sawdust. I struggled to my feet and stepped over to my stall door. Thankfully, I was far enough away from the barn door so only my human half could be seen from her angle. I sucked up what was left of my sanity. "Aunt Bonnie, please don't come any closer. I've got to tell . . . got to explain. . .something. . ."

"Thank God you're alright! What are you doing here? You should be home. Jerry, what's going on?" She came two steps closer down the aisle.

"I've had . . .I got. . . a sort of accident. . ." I fumbled. I gave up trying to come up with the right words, shoved the stall door open, and stepped out into the aisle.

Her mouth dropped open and the bucket fell from her hand with a loud bang, rolling towards Gold Coast's stall. Her eyes were wide and her jaws worked, trying to form words. Finally, she got out. "By the gods of Olympus . . .what happened?"

"I don't know," I moaned. "I thought you might be able to help figure it out. I'm just glad you don't think I'm a monster."

She ran to me and hugged me around my human torso, patting my back. I tried my best not to cry as I bent to return her hug, so glad she understood. She drew back, kissed me on the cheek, and looked me over. "You are my nephew, no matter what. We will figure this out."

I finally noticed my horse part was as black as ebony with white socks all around. She then walked around me, ran her hand down my horse side, and checked my legs and hooves. This all felt really strange.

"You look healthy after that fall in the kitchen. I called your dad last night when I saw the police car at your house, and now the kitchen disaster makes sense. God knows this change and all must be traumatic. Can you tell me everything that happened that you remember over the last day or so while I see to my morning chores? They're not going to do it themselves. Chores will help me think. Do a lot of mystery plotting while I work," she said, coming around to face me again.

"I can help with chores," I offered.

She winked. "I can handle it. You just try to relax. Tell me what happened."

Everything that happened since I left after our game on Wednesday came spilling out. She paused several times in her feeding and watering to ponder what I said and did allow me to push the wheelbarrow from stall to stall as she forked out the droppings. She seemed to take it all in with no problem in accepting it.

Every horse in the barn had its head over their stall doors and seemed quite interested in me, too. Gold Coast even stuck his head out far enough to sniff at my hip before he tried to bite me on the butt as I passed his stall.

When Aunt Bonnie finished, closed the feed room door, and looked over at me. I froze. She had a thoughtful expression on her face. "You know, I wish I could get a look at the stone Andrew Collins threw into the cornfield. It reminds me of a *D&D* module I played back in college."

I suddenly had the terrible urge to pee. I was totally embarrassed by a certain part of my horse anatomy. "Aunt Bonnie, I have to . . ."

She just matter-of-factly waved her hand at me. "Go use your stall. Pick a corner where you won't bed down. You'll never fit in the bathroom. Just remember to lift your tail out of the way and lean your hips slightly forward. Don't be embarrassed. The horse part is new to you. Just think of the good thing about it; you can go anywhere and don't need a bathroom."

"But it's embarrassing," I protested and rushed to my stall, feeling my face go red regardless of what she said. "I'm going to have to read up on centaurs in the *D&D* books, too."

"Studying the Greek myths is better, though not that much is mentioned about centaurs," she said as she took the wheelbarrow out to dump it and returned to put it in the corner where she kept it. "It was recorded there was a herd of centaurs in the forest in ancient Thessaly. Centaurs were known to be magic shapeshifters, teachers of the Hellenic gods, healers, and practice divination and astronomy. Yet they were violent, lusty drunks if they overindulged.

"They can be warlike and are deadly with the bow, spear, or club. The most famous was Chiron, the teacher of Greek heroes. The source of the myth itself is thought to be derived from Hindu Ashvins, the man-horse wizards of central Asia of the horse culture tribes of the East. You must admit the first time a mounted warrior was seen by Western cultures had to be a frightening experience."

"We didn't cover that in school or meet any in *D & D* yet." I left my stall.

"Today centaurs do, on occasion, show up in popular books and movies like *The Lion, the Witch and the Wardrobe*, *Harry Potter*, and the *Percy Jackson and the Olympians* series as one of the good guys. Like I said, they are rather rare."

Aunt Bonnie's words did not help all that much. I knew I needed to hide until we could find how to reverse whatever it was that did this to me.

"My whole life is ruined. . . I can't go home . . . I can't go to school. I can just imagine the reaction of Andrew and his Neanderthals. The Homeland Security people and black ops will be after me. . ." I was working myself into a full-blown panic attack.

"Easy, Jerry. No one is going to know yet. You can stay here with me and we'll work this out. I do have some good news about all this. Yesterday afternoon I closed on the thirty-five acres of wood between my place and yours. Harry Thomas, up in Lexington, didn't want to hold on to it any longer and my new bestselling novel, *Mystery at Black Jack Key,* provided a nice down payment. I want it so I can brush hog a trail through it that my boarders can use instead of riding along the county road.

"For now, it can be part of your living space rather than being cooped up here in the barn and risk discovery by my boarders. You and I can build a nice shelter," she said, putting her hand on my human back. "We'll solve this and the more I think about it, the more I believe we've got to find the stone that jock threw into the cornfield. I'm sure it's the key."

"We can try tonight when it gets dark," I said, feeling better. "If the stone still glows, it should be easy to find."

"Keep those good thoughts while I go make breakfast. You must be hungry. I have plenty of pancake mix and a bunch of sausages. How's that sound?" she asked with a devilish smile.

"Perfect!"

"Good. Now while it's still dark, go out down to the woods and wait. I'll be joining you as soon as I cook up a big breakfast. Can't chance your sister coming by to check on Gold Coast or any of the other owners showing up." Aunt Bonnie patted my right horse shoulder.

"Good idea." I followed her out of the barn into the early morning first light that turned the rolling farmland to shades of gray.

4

The Hut, the Fall, and the Stone

I galloped through Aunt Bonnie's pasture toward the woods she now owned. With no gate in the four-foot-high wire and post fence, I dared to jump in and, by some miracle, made it over. In fact, I sailed over it as if it was not even there. It was a great feat for me since I'm not on the track team and far from athletic.

However, I knew it had more to do with the "new" horse part of me. I'd have to get rid of my old notions of what I could and could not do physically. I walked slowly along the edge of the woods, checking it out for about an hour by my watch. The whole forest was a mix of deciduous trees just beginning to leaf out with a few pines and appeared quite thick with sprouting green undergrowth and spring wildflowers in sunny patches. I heard a babbling stream somewhere out in the dying darkness.

I know thirty-five acres was not all that much land, but it looked like a good, out of the way place to lay low until we could solve this whole mess. I intended to explore more, but the sound of Aunt Bonnie's John

Deere Gator RSX utility vehicle headed my way postponed my mission.

She stopped by the fence and called out, "Jerry, come and get it."

I trotted out of the woods to find her dishing out a stack of six hot pancakes and eight sausage patties onto a platter she took from a wicker basket on the passenger side of the front seat.

When she noticed me approaching, she asked, "Honey or real maple syrup?"

"Honey."

She poured a lot of honey over the stack and passed the plate and a fork over the fence to me when I reached her.

"I've got to get a gate installed here, but not until you have a shelter. We'll explore the land and start that project after breakfast. There's another dozen pancakes in the basket still warm and in foil, so don't be shy about asking for more." She dished out three for herself and ate along with me. When we finished eating, we shared a thermos of rich coffee.

As she drank hers, she looked off toward my house. Then she turned to me with a serious, motherly look. "You know, as soon as possible we should tell the rest of our family what happened. I talked to your mom a moment ago on the phone, and she is devastated by your disappearance. Both your parents and I were questioned by a couple of detectives until one this morning."

I knew this subject would be brought up sooner or later. Guilt clutched at my throat, and I looked at the ground as if it held an answer. I croaked, "I just don't think they'll understand. Magic is not part of their reality."

"I don't think they will reject you. You are their son. Flesh of their flesh, as the old saying goes."

"I don't know. . . What about Ann? She'll freak quicker than anyone even though she likes horses. Our worlds are far apart as it is; her with her horsey friends and shows and me into physics, *D&D,* and all."

"She is trying to be brave, but she refused to go to school today and keeps asking why the police don't turn up clues. Oh, by the way, the detectives will be coming back to search your yard this morning with a K-9 unit. Your bedroom and kitchen have been declared crime scenes. Last night the detectives did an evidence sweep of the upstairs hall and stairs, too, from what your mom said."

I sighed. "You know the only things they will find out of the ordinary are horse hairs and the scratches on the floor and furniture matching the unshod hooves of a horse. If they figure that out . . ."

"It will confuse them. But the upside is when they inform your family, the strange evidence will make them more accepting of your condition, as crazy as that sounds. It will not change the need to find the stone. I believe some kind of true magic is at work here. Now, let's find a spot in these woods to create a shelter to keep you dry and comfortable."

When we finished with breakfast, Aunt Bonnie collected the dirty dishes and flatware and put them in the basket. Then she bent over and ducked between the fence wires to reach my side.

"Let's trace down that brook first," she suggested.

We hiked along a deer trail and found a narrow brook, hardly a yard wide that meandered through the woods about a hundred yards from the border of our cornfield. It ran through a large stand of young maples and ash trees with a lot of undergrowth almost reaching the banks.

"This is great," Aunt Bonnie said. "I have one of those water purification straws from wilderness camping. I'll bring it and a clean bucket later and you will have a safe source of water. I know this little brook is spring fed from the plate of the property the realtor gave me."

"That's one worry gone, but I hope I will not be camping out here long after tonight. We've got to find that stone," I returned. The urgency had me in a death grip.

"I agree, but we still must be prepared if we don't find it as quick as we wish. We only have a general idea of where the stone landed. Plus, we still have to figure out the connection between it and your transformation; the how and why of it all," Aunt Bonnie continued.

My thoughts retreated to the scientific method of solving a mystery: ask a question, make a hypothesis, conduct an experiment, record the results, draw a conclusion. "I bet it's cursed or something," I added, thinking out loud. "Andrew called me a horse's ass while holding that stone and now I have one."

Aunt Bonnie shrugged. "I think you may be right about that. Now, let's find a good site for a shelter. Besides breakfast, I brought a large tarp to keep rain out, a spool of heavy twine to secure it, plus the big toolbox with the hacksaw."

We continued walking, following deer trails away from the brook. I found myself memorizing the lay of the land into a mental map. In an area covered by mosses, ferns, and saplings the forest opened up into a smaller meadow of perhaps an acre.

"These saplings will be perfect," Aunt Bonnie announced. "We can bend them into a frame for a wigwam type shelter, cut other branches to weave between them to reinforce the structure into an upside-down basket shape. Then we can use the tarp as a weatherproof roof and pile brush on it for camouflage. I'll bring up some sawdust bales for bedding, and it should be quite comfortable with a couple of quilts and a pillow."

We hiked back to the Gator to retrieve our supplies and got to work on the construction. By the middle of the afternoon, I had a nice hut. But work only kept my mind occupied for a short time.

When Aunt Bonnie went back to see to her afternoon barn chores and dinner, I was left alone with my worries. I needed to look out at my house to see what was going on in the life I was missing with my family and still remain hidden.

I explored the edge of the woods under the cover of laurel and witch hazel shrubs and found a low hill from which I could view both properties yet remain unseen in the sparse spring vegetation. I must admit I could see Aunt Bonnie's two arenas better than my house, but I could see enough beyond the cornfield to spot two cars in the driveway I could not identify and it bothered me. I figured it probably belonged to a police detective and the K-9 handler.

I noticed Ann leading Gold Coast from the barn to the arena where jumps were set up. I wished I had binoculars so I could get a closer view of Ann to gauge her emotions, yet I knew she was throwing herself into jump practice to keep from fretting over my disappearance. Riding was her "safe place" like gaming was mine. I decided to watch her though, as I often went to her horse shows.

I already knew she was a member of both the US Equestrian Federation and the subsidiary United States Hunter Jumper Association, including being a USEF High School Letter Athlete. Plus, had won championships in the fifteen to seventeen-year-old sections of jumper and equitation and was poised for a serious run to become a part of the U. S. Equestrian team and Olympics in the future. She and Gold Coast were in perfect sync, held show jumping certification, and he was like an extended member of the family. To me he was sort of like a big dog.

See, I'm not a true horse person like my sister, though that sounds like a stupid statement considering what's happened. But I was not into her sport any more than she was into my gaming. I showed up at her shows more or less for moral support. Oh, I had more victories in my own way, like winning the science fairs all the way to state and national levels, but that hardly got a nod or acknowledgment from her.

The arena was set up as a course of various jumps. I knew they all had special names but never bothered to learn them. To me, the scariest one was a high rail fence with a lower one right next to it.

The low one was on the approach side and a mistake in judgment by either the horse or rider could be disastrous. Stadium jumping was not for the faint of heart once a rider and horse hit the more advanced classes. I saw a few nasty accidents at the shows.

There were a variety of eight jumps in the arena Aunt Bonnie had built to the regulations set by the United States Equestrian Federation. One was even a water jump consisting of a fence in the middle of a twelve-foot-long rectangular pool about a foot deep.

I settled at my secret vantage point to observe, though my mind kept wandering back to the other night when that brain-dead jock Andrew threw my stone into the cornfield. I tried to remember the exact spot I saw the landing so we could find it without too much effort.

My eyes followed Ann and Gold Coast while I pondered the stone's location.

At the last jump, one of those two unequal fence combinations, everything in our lives came to a terrible screeching halt. Gold Coast must have clipped the fence with a front hoof or something. The upper rail fell. He stumbled on it and went down on his front knees, throwing Ann clear over his head.

My heart jumped into my throat and breath caught in my lungs. Immediately, Aunt Bonnie ran from the stable to the arena. Ann got up slowly and limped to Gold Coast as he untangled himself from the fallen rails.

He seemed to be favoring his right front leg. Aunt Bonnie grabbed the reins first as Ann reached them and gave the reins to her. Then Aunt Bonnie checked the leg and got out her iPhone.

Ann rubbed Gold Coast's face and pressed her own against his cheek. Her face was red, and I was sure she was crying. I could only watch helplessly. It hurt not to be able to do a thing for them. Next thing I knew, they led Gold Coast to the barn and stopped to run water from the outside hose attached to the pump over his leg, from his knee down to his hoof.

I left my observation spot, determined to get closer. I galloped through the woods to a point where the trees closely skirted the pasture fence and stopped within fifty yards of the jumping arena. Keeping underbrush and a few thick pine trees between me and the arena, I crept as close as I dared, careful not to step on any fallen branches or rustle the bushes.

In about fifteen minutes or so, Dr. Pratt, our local large animal vet, arrived in his van that was stocked as a mini clinic right down to having a portable x-ray and ultra-sound. Though I could not hear the words that passed between them, I did see Ann was crying by her frequent efforts to brush away tears. Dr. Pratt got right to work with Aunt Bonnie assisting. It all looked grave from where I stood. The three of them took Gold Coast into the barn.

I was determined to ask Aunt Bonnie how serious the injury was when I saw her for dinner. I knew all too well Ann's dream of that big jumping competition was more than likely doomed along with the rest of her summer show plans, unless she could somehow get a replacement. The Cross-County Hunter Jumper Horse Show was only six weeks away.

I headed for my hut to wait for Aunt Bonnie at that point. I was feeling even worse over the miserable compounding of our family disasters and just wanted to hide from the world. I could not help but think Ann's attention was not fully focused on taking that last jump because of being distracted by worry over my disappearance. She misjudged the distance and the accident resulted.

Aunt Bonnie showed up at my hut around twilight with a bucket of KFC chicken and a family serving of mashed potatoes.

"Did not have time to cook dinner. Guess you may have seen what happened." She handed me the meal.

"Yes, and it's my fault," I said miserably. "She was probably distracted by worrying about me. How bad is Gold Coast hurt?"

"The ultrasound showed a torn suspensory branch ligament. He will recover, but it will mean six to nine months of rest and three months of retraining, depending on how well he recovers. Ann will be sleeping in the barn tonight. Dr. Pratt gave him a shot for pain and a mild sedative to keep him quiet, plus wrapped his leg for support…"

"Will we still be able to hunt for the stone?" I asked, feeling it a bad show of ego though it would cure part of a family disaster.

"You will have to hunt alone and be extremely careful. I'll be staying with Ann in the barn tonight. Dr. Pratt will be by about 10 a.m. to check on him again. Make sure you stay in the woods and out of sight."

What little optimism I had went right down the drain. I sighed. "That kills the odds of finding it quickly," I complained. "But I'll be back in the woods before dawn."

"We'll try again tomorrow night together. I don't think I'll have the time to search during the day with everything that is going on. Don't give up," she returned. "Eat your dinner. I'll see you early tomorrow morning with breakfast."

I nodded and she left me standing there by the hut as she made her way back to the pasture by way of the deer trail. Though I did not originally feel hungry, the second I opened the KFC bucket of chicken, and the familiar smell of the spices hit me, I found myself ravenous. I ate everything Aunt Bonnie brought, leaving only the bare bones in the bucket.

When it was dark, I made my way to our cornfield through the woods. The new green leaves had just started to come up, looking like giant crabgrass. Dad had planted it on April 15th. Once at the edge of the field, I decided the best way to tackle the search in a methodical manner was to walk between the rows and poke my hooves in the dirt to see if I could hit the stone if it was not glowing.

I started at about the middle of the row bordering Aunt Bonnie's front yard. Though I thought I knew about where it fell, it could have bounced on soft earth or another stone in a different direction. It was very slow going.

There was no sign of a glowing stone. Frustration built. I kicked over dirt clods, nudged around new weeds, and froze every time a car came down the road. Though my *Star Wars* t-shirt was black, I dared not get too close to the road for fear someone's high headlight beam might catch me.

A rider on a headless horse would definitely cause a stir and probably get me into the local Civil War ghost lore. Aunt Bonnie would have to search close to the road. I gave up before midnight only a third of the way toward where the stone might be and headed back to my hut. The little sleep I got that night was fitful.

5
Reunion, Oxers, and Hogsbacks

At three Saturday morning, I woke up from a nightmare of being chased by a black helicopter through the woods. My t-shirt was soaked with sweat despite the chilly night. I threw off the quilt, rolled over and got up, miserable. I wondered if I would ever get back to my normal life again, even if that meant constant badgering by the jocks until I went to college.

My distraught thoughts dredged up Aunt Bonnie's words. "You know, as soon as possible we should tell our family what happened."

Maybe, just maybe, she might be right, I told myself, staring at the sky outside my hut door.

I would not have to go far to start. Ann was in the barn and Aunt Bonnie could back me up if things got crazy. They could let our parents know. The news coming from both of them might soften the shock. It was worth a try. I sucked up what shreds of my courage were left and headed out of my hut to walk to the barn in the moonlight. I relied on my excellent night vision, a centaur trait I was glad to have, as screwed up as my life had just become.

To keep from talking myself out of revealing myself to Ann, I jumped the fence, galloped across the pasture, and only slowed at the gate to let myself through. I was a lot more careful in my approach to the barn door.

Upon reaching it, I got down on my knees to make my height seem more normal and slid the door on its track open far enough to peek in. Aunt Bonnie had set up two camping cots in the aisle, and they were sitting on them talking to one another. Their heads both snapped around to face me the second the door creaked on its track.

Ann jumped up on her feet and screamed out, "Jerry!" She ran at me.

"Don't come any closer!" I shouted.

She stopped short, confused. "Why?

"Something has happened. I've changed. It's all a strange accident. Real Twilight Zone stuff."

Aunt Bonnie joined her, putting her hands on Ann's shoulders. "I'm glad you decided to come forward, Jerry. You will need all our support to get through this."

Ann looked from me to Aunt Bonnie and back to me, confused and worried. "Aunt Bonnie, what the hell is going on? You're scaring me. Jerry, are you hurt?"

"Not exactly," I said, got off my knees, pushed the door open all the way, and stepped into the glare of the fluorescent lights. Some of the boarders nickered.

Ann sucked in her breath sharply, her eyes widened and both her hands covered her mouth.

"Aunt Bonnie and I are trying to figure it all out. You can see why I could not stay home or let anyone know when my bed crashed and I woke up like this," I said.

Next, I knew, Ann broke away from Aunt Bonnie, rushed me crying and hugged me around where my human waist joined the horse shoulders. When she got control, she wiped her eyes and looked up at me.

Her words spilled out like a torrent. "I don't know what to say except we got to let Mom and Dad know. They are beside themselves. Think you were kidnapped or something. The police are baffled by the evidence. Now the horsehair and hoof marks make sense. God, how did this happen?" She turned away to look over at Aunt Bonnie for an answer.

"We are not sure, but suspect it has something to do with a glowing stone he found Wednesday evening," Aunt Bonnie answered.

"That's your crazy *Dungeons and Dragon* stuff. Magic is not real," Ann shot back in total classic denial.

"Then how do you explain me? This is not a costume!" I stamped my left front hoof and switched my tail.

Ann stared at me like a deer in the headlights as if seeing me for the first time. She slowly reached her hand out to touch my horse shoulder. I twitched the muscle like horses do to get rid of flies. She pulled her hand away and stepped back, a look of alarm and resignation in her eyes.

"It's real . . . Oh . . . My . . . God!"

"We need to find the stone. That jock Andrew threw it into our cornfield Wednesday night when he took it from me and called me a real horse's ass. Now I have one. The stone has to be cursed. That's all we know," I explained. "It's a theory."

Gold Coast chose that moment to hang his head over his stall door and nicker, breaking into our heavy drama.

"Sorry about what happened to Gold Coast," I said. "I saw the accident. Aunt Bonnie told me what the vet said."

She nodded and her tears began to flow again. She brushed them away. "We got to tell our parents about you. We just got to. Summer is ruined as it is. Our lives are ruined . . . and all because of that brain-dead jock Andrew."

I stepped over and hugged her.

"Let's wait until morning and Ann and I can bring them over. Jerry, you take the empty box stall," Aunt Bonnie said. "We have to plan this carefully to ease the trauma as best as we can."

"I don't think it's too bad now that the shock is over. Jerry, you make a real nice horse," Ann said as a tremulous smile broke through her tears.

"Centaur, Ann. I am a centaur," I corrected her and let her go. "You know, half man and half horse like in *The Lion, the Witch, and the Wardrobe* and *Harry Potter* and . . ."

"You know I really don't think they will be all that traumatized once the first shock is over. I mean, you're not dead or maimed. You're part black stallion." Ann went to sit on the cot closest to Gold Coast and looked back at me kind of strange, part pleading and part covetous manner as she rubbed Gold Coast's nose.

"Don't you tell anyone else about me. Especially your horsey girlfriends." I walked past Aunt Bonnie and Ann to the stall. "I know how teen girls like to gossip. I could end up in a lab, or worse."

"He's right," Aunt Bonnie agreed. "This does not go outside this family without agreement of all."

"Okay," Ann grumbled with the slightest of pouts and laid back on her cot.

I walked into my stall and Aunt Bonnie turned off the lights, leaving just a night light on. I had trouble falling asleep. My mind was running at light speed, envisioning how things might go later in the morning when our parents came over. I just hoped Ann was right.

After looking to feeding her chickens and boarders first thing before dawn with our help, Aunt Bonnie and Ann headed to our house. One good thing; no one would be rushing off to work with it being the weekend.

They were gone a whole hour before I heard Dad's KIA Sorento coming up the drive toward the stable. I returned to my stall and stood, leaning my crossed arms on the closed stall door ledge. Four car doors opened and slammed.

"I wish you two did not make this such a mystery, Sis." I heard my father say.

"I told you he is fine. Just changed. It is best you look and know it is not a joke or a trick," Aunt Bonnie returned, and pulled open the barn door along its track. "Just stop inside and let Jerry explain."

My parents rushed in with Ann and Aunt Bonnie following and stopped short when I waved from the stall. "Hi."

They could only see the upper part of my normal half.

"What's going on, Jerry?" Dad demanded.

"Jerry, why all the secrecy?" Mom started.

"Don't freak," I interrupted. "This is not easy for me and I don't know what happened. We are still trying to figure it all out."

Aunt Bonnie closed the barn door behind everyone and nodded at me. I pushed the stall door open and stepped out. My parents' shocked looks hit like a tsunami. Then a massive group hug hit with equal force.

"You should have come back to us yesterday morning!" Mom cried, sniffing back tears.

"In this condition and with the police poking around?" I returned.

"It would not have mattered with us after the initial shock wore off and we could have called the police to tell them not to come since you returned unharmed," Dad said. "You are our son, and Bonnie explained things the best she could without telling the whole truth. However, as a scientist, I just can't quite believe the magic aspect of it. This kind of transmutation is. . . is . . . must be in some kind of quantum physical realm we have not yet discovered."

"Well, science was once thought to be magic. And there was once in medical science experiments to mix and create new species like four-legged chickens and ape men that were called chimeras."

We all released each other. I stared at them and they stared at me.

Behind them, Ann laughed. "This is so awesome!"

"Well, if it helps, think of the physics part of it. There are supposed to be other dimensions. We may just live in a Multiverse instead of a Universe. That stone could have come from another dimension."

There was dead silence for a moment.

"Jerry, you could be right." Dad patted my human shoulder. He turned to the rest of the family. "Some of us in astrophysics say there are twenty-one dimensions. Others say there are more all touching each other like soap bubbles with thin skins as barriers."

Aunt Bonnie chimed in, "Something could have happened; maybe a portal to a dimension where magic is part of reality. All legends have a basis in fact. Or so say anthropologists."

Mom spoke up. "What about this stone you found?"

"It's out in the cornfield someplace. I tried to find it. Aunt Bonnie thinks it might have had something to do with it all," I answered. "This happened after I was called a horse's ass by Andrew who got it away from me, and threw it into our cornfield."

"What did it look like?" Dad asked, an expression of genuine interest sparkling in his eyes.

"Like a moonstone about the size of a half dollar, glass smooth, and it glowed like foxfire."

"I would be very cautious about handling it if we do find it," Aunt Bonnie warned. "And, if we do, we have to find out how we can use it to bring Jerry back to normal, if that is possible. It will take some experimentation, not to mention keeping it from people who might also want it if news gets out. Once we get Jerry back, it should be destroyed in my humble opinion."

A frown flitted over my father's face. "Let's not race to judgment."

"I can't wait much longer. I have to finish school. Take exams and . . ." I started.

"Home schooling online," Mom broke in. "I'll arrange it on Monday."

"And, before you do that, we have to inform the police Jerry is back and okay. Come up with a logical story," Dad said.

"How about a story of a mystery hazing by unknowns that dumped him in the Daniel Boone National Forest? You got a call and went down to get him. Let's hope they don't come to check it out," Aunt Bonnie suggested, her plotting mystery writer's mind probably in overdrive.

"Sounds good enough. I can also tell them he is too traumatized to talk to them until the doctor says he can. I'll figure out something to keep them away from here, as much as I hate lying. This is a family emergency." Dad frowned again.

"And what about getting out and exercise? My horse part needs exercise. I know that from Ann and her horsy friends. And what about my friends? My whole freaking life is ruined," I moaned.

Everyone's face went solemn like at a funeral.

Ann spoke up. "For exercise you can go work out in the evening over the jumps. I can teach you all about them, the oxer double jump, the hogsback, and more. Somebody ought to get use of them besides the one boarder, my friend and jumping coach, Mrs. Albert, who is involved in jumping horse shows and judging for the local chapter of the United States Equestrian Federation. I certainly won't be using them for a long while." She looked despondently over at Gold Coast nibbling hay in his stall.

I knew she was hurting deeply over his injury. It distressed me to see her so upset.

"Sounds like a plan," Aunt Bonnie said. "You can hardly see the jumping arena from the road, since part of my apple orchard blocks the view."

Their words made me feel a bit better. "But what about my friends? They need game night to keep their sanity and will be worried where I disappeared to and—"

"I'll still have the games for them and will feel them out on the situation. If all goes well and I believe they can be trusted to keep a secret, we may have a reunion and move the games to this barn. Meanwhile, I'm going to spend the rest of the morning looking for that stone."

"I'll join you," Dad said.

"So will I," Mom interjected. "I'll cancel my ten o'clock showing of the Paterson place."

"I'll join, too, since I won't be doing any practice with Gold Coast," Ann added.

"Waffles okay for breakfast?" Aunt Bonnie asked. "I'll bring a big batch over shortly with honey and maple syrup. We have to finish quickly and before Dr. Pratt gets here at 10 a.m."

We all agreed. I was feeling a strong case of the warm fuzzies when everyone else crowded around me after Aunt Bonnie headed for the house.

Ann decided I could do with a good grooming, grabbed some brushes and handed them out to our parents, showing Dad the proper way to use them. She took a comb to my tail to get out the tangles. It was all very strange, wonderful, and a little embarrassing, all rolled into one. Still, I hoped someone would find that stone sooner rather than later.

6
Hurdles

When Aunt Bonnie returned with her picnic basket full of waffles and the rest of our breakfast, she also brought me binoculars in a case.

"These are my bird watching glasses, but they are good enough for you to keep an eye on our stone hunt and for other observations." She handed the case to me.

All through breakfast, both my parents and Ann kept looking over at me surreptitiously. In a way, it bothered me. It reminded me of a dream I once had of showing up at school in only my underwear.

When she finished eating, Mom said, "I'm going to bring you more of your t-shirts later and put that one in the wash. I'll also bring your black hoodie sweatshirt in case we are due for a cold night. Is there anything else you'd like?"

"I'd like my life back, but you already know that. How about my iPhone?" My warm fuzzy feeling was melting.

I still wanted to contact Ben and Alice and hoped I could convince my family to allow it. I knew they would understand and not be afraid of the transmutation. We were all *D&D* geeks and used to myths and the critters that occupied them.

"Contacting your friends now may not be a good idea," Dad warned, as if reading my mind. "Let Aunt Bonnie break it to them on game night, if she feels they can handle it. Then, we'll see."

"But they need to know I'm still alive. It's not fair to keep them in the dark and in a constant state of worry and stress. Exam time is stressful enough," I explained. "They need closure. Especially when my kidnapping hits the local newspaper or other media."

"I don't have to lecture you on the fact that life is not fair, do I?" he shot back.

I frowned. "No. I'm living proof."

"Let's get on that hunt for the stone," Mom broke in. "We don't need to stray into a philosophical debate right now."

Not long after Mom's great referee move, they all trooped out of the barn, and I headed out to the pasture. It was already getting light. I hurried through the gate, galloped across the pasture and jumped the fence into the woods, sailing over it as if I had wings. I'd find out later that jumping within sight of my sister was a mistake.

I took up a position on that low hill and watched the search through the binoculars, very glad to have them. I kept the case slung diagonally over my shoulder so it hung within easy reach where my human hip would have been, and the case now leaned against my horse shoulder.

The search for the stone went on most of the morning. Ann and Aunt Bonnie only broke away when

Dr. Pratt arrived at 10:00 a.m. They were back in a half hour. Observing the search was about as exciting as watching an archaeological dig.

Around noon, Aunt Bonnie suddenly stopped Dad from touching something on the ground with his hand not far from where I thought the stone had landed. She ran to her house. In moments, she came running back with rubber gloves, oven mitts, BBQ tongs, and a small metal box stuffed with what looked like paper towels. She put on the rubber gloves, then the oven mitts, and appeared to carefully pick something off the ground with the tongs and deposit it in the box.

When they all started toward the barn, I headed down from my vantage point to a thick stand of saplings where the deer trail started near the pasture fence. There I found Mom, Dad, and Ann following Aunt Bonnie through the pasture with broad smiles on their faces.

Aunt Bonnie ducked through the fence with the open box in hands still covered in the oven mitts as I walked over toward them. Mom had the tongs.

Aunt Bonnie asked, "Is this the stone?"

I looked at it. In the daylight it did not appear to be glowing, but it was a moonstone of the right size with a silvery glint. "It looks like it, only it's not glowing."

"Let's try something. Pick it up and wish to be human. Words have power in the magical realm. Choose your words carefully, just like in our games," Aunt Bonnie cautioned.

With everyone looking on and holding their breath, I cautiously took the stone in my right hand. "I wish to be back in my human body as Gerald Swift, age seventeen."

It abruptly gave me an electric shock as if someone had used a taser on my hand and quickly became too hot to hold.

"Ow!" I bellowed and dropped it, shook my hand, and blew on it.

Nothing happened. I was still a centaur.

"You, okay?" Mom yelled, rushing the fence.

"It shocked and burned me. That's all," I replied, looking at a red spot on my palm.

She ducked through the fence to have a look for herself. Aunt Bonnie picked up the stone with the oven mitt and deposited it back in the box on its cushion of paper towels and closed the lid. "Apparently it only works one way."

"What am I going to do?" I moaned. "I can't stay like this forever."

"Let me take it to our lab at the university and have it analyzed. If it came from another dimension, it might have a different molecular signature and could be the proof we need, not to mention the biggest discovery this century. Then maybe we can use it to find the dimensional portal where it originated," Dad said, reaching over the fence for the box.

"I don't think that is a very good idea." Aunt Bonnie pulled it out of his reach. "It's obvious you have to be extremely careful what you say around it. Lab techs would laugh at that order and be stupid enough to call you or someone else something just to be funny and we'll have another problem.

"Or your science department heads may even want to see what happened to Jerry, ship it and Jerry off to some government lab, and we'll never see them again. I'm going to put this in a safe place where no one will get at it while we figure how to get Jerry back to normal."

"That is very unscientific of you, Bonnie. Never took you to believe in fairy tales or sorcery," Dad snapped, frowning.

"This has nothing to do with science. This is magic, pure and simple, which puts it in the realm of metaphysics." She ducked under the wire to head for her house, still carrying the box with Dad following her. They started arguing about the nature of magic and physics, but were quickly out of hearing range.

"So sorry, honey," Mom said, hugged and kissed me, turned and ducked under the wire to follow them.

Ann stayed behind, looking me over critically as if I were a horse at an auction. There was a strange expression in her eyes that girls get when they are thinking deeply about something they want, but don't want to ask about at the moment. "Are you going to try the jumps in the arena tonight for exercise?"

"Maybe," I said, feeling frustration rise like magma. "It depends how I feel. Right now, I'd like to be alone."

I left her standing by the pasture fence and trotted down the deer trail toward my hut. Satisfied she was not following; I explored the thirty-five-acre woods the rest of the morning, contemplating my life and trying not to get depressed. The stone only seemed to work one way as a curse. Was it a temporary curse with an expiration date or was this change permanent?

Maybe Aunt Bonnie should have let Dad take the stone to the lab even with all the risks. Other thoughts hit. If it came from another dimension, was it stolen? And if so, was someone looking for it? What was its purpose? My whole life had suddenly turned into a real *D&D* adventure.

My stomach growled. I looked at my watch. It was almost one. I trekked to the edge of my woods by the pasture when I heard Aunt Bonnie's Gator approaching. I watched her stop and get out of it.

"Jerry, lunch!" she immediately called out.

I caught her smile as I trotted over to the fence.

"I have a whole basket full of peanut butter and jelly sandwiches from your mom, bottles of iced tea, a carton of chocolate milk, and half a dozen apples. Plus, that filter straw to use at the spring. Your mom also sent a plastic bag of a dozen of your t-shirts and the hoodie." She took everything out of the Gator and passed it over the fence to me. "She would have come, but she had a client show up all the way from New York, and no one else was available in the office. Your dad went over to the college. Don't worry. I did not give him the stone. I hid it in my college trunk up in the attic. It's safe for now."

"Thanks," I said blandly. I was trying to not feel sorry for myself, but was quickly spiraling down into depression. I felt I had hit a brick wall in solving this whole mess.

"Monday morning, I have Joe from Blackwell Construction coming over to install a gate right here, so you will have to keep out of sight. Tonight, before dark, feel free to use the jumping arena. I have the arena lights on an automatic timer. Ann will probably be there after she walks Gold Coast a little to keep him from losing muscle tone. You exercising in the arena was all she could talk about with us before going off to the movies with friends to catch the early show."

"I hope she doesn't blab about me to her horsey friends now or Monday," I complained. I was beginning to see where this all might be leading in her mind and did not like it one bit. I had the disconcerting feeling she was considering me to replace Gold Coast. That was the height of insanity, but I knew all too well desperate situations often called for desperate solutions, especially in the teen mind and she would probably put me on the biggest guilt trip of my life. "Have you any idea what happened to me and how to solve it?"

"Well, at this point, to be honest, nothing outside of some kind of curse. However, I plan on going up into my attic and finding that other trunk I put more of my *D&D* game modules in from college. I saved everything. I half remember an adventure dealing with a lot of different magic jewels set in Ancient Greece and if I can find it, I'm going to read through it to see if I get another clue. Some of the writers based their game module stories on real legends."

I sighed. "Well, I guess that's something. See you later."

I headed off to my hut as Aunt Bonnie drove off in her Gator. I ate everything Mom packed. I left the shirts in the plastic bag hanging from a section of branch in my hut that was off the ground to keep them from getting damp from the humidity. I still wished I had my iPhone to call Alice and Ben. I felt isolated. Maybe exiled is a better word.

I took a nap in a sunny spot for most of the afternoon and was awakened by a Carolina wren pulling hairs out of my tail for nest construction. I moved my tail and the tiny bird took off with several long hairs in its beak. The sun was getting below its zenith. It was three by my watch.

Bored out of my mind, I headed to my observation point to check my house and Aunt Bonnie's barn and arenas with the binoculars. I must admit, it was like a stakeout in a police drama but being unable to make contact with my friends with my iPhone, spying was the only way I could keep up with my real world.

The second I reached my observation post; I saw motion in the jump arena and looked through the binoculars. Mrs. Albert was exercising her chestnut mare

Drama Queen over the jumps, and Ann was leaning on the fence watching her.

My heart jumped, too.

I hoped Ann was not talking about anything to do with me. Mrs. Albert had boarded her mare with Aunt Bonnie for four years and often gave my sister pointers on her riding technique. They were quite close and Ann looked up to her as a mentor, talking of her often over dinner. She was a slim woman in her forties with red hair and a bubbly personality, who, if I remembered right also had something to do with the Olympics.

My mind was usually on other things when Ann talked about her horsey friends, and I only half heard her. That was even more of a reason enough to believe she was thinking of doing something crazy now seeing them together.

I knew I should just ask Ann point blank, "Are you trying to guilt me into taking Gold Coast's place as long as I am stuck being a centaur?" It's more than suspicion over a growing body of circumstantial evidence. Centaurs are supposed to have the gift of precognition – be able to predict the future – or at least some could.

Perhaps I was developing that skill. Perhaps the longer I stayed in this new body, the more like the legendary centaurs I would become. But I could not see myself being a rowdy drunk.

I watched Mrs. Albert take Drama Queen over the jumps, observing closely how she did it. If I was going to use them for exercise, I needed to learn the proper form used to take each jump in a safe manner. This was like track and field for horses.

In a way, I was fascinated by the challenge of this other new world. Drama Queen seemed to fly over the jumps like Pegasus without wings. Together they were a thing of beauty to watch working as if of one mind.

When Mrs. Albert finished her workout and walked her mare to cool her down, Ann joined her. I watched, wishing I could read lips. When they headed around the other side of the barn, my suspicions rose. Drama Queen was taken back into the barn and a short time later; Mrs. Albert got into her car with Ann and left.

I shifted the binoculars to face my house. Mrs. Albert pulled up and she and Ann went into the house. I about had a fit. Something was up. I just knew it. A feeling of betrayal swept through me.

I felt like a fool to even think my metamorphosis could have been kept secret. I felt as if I was on the verge of becoming a legend like Big Foot and starting to attract unwanted attention.

The voice of reason pushed through the turmoil of my outrage. Maybe, just maybe, Ann had asked Mrs. Albert if she could borrow Drama Queen for the summer events. If so, there would be official paperwork that had to be done for substitutions.

Plus, a new jumping certificate of capability for both horse and rider like I remember she did with Gold Coast every year. Mrs. Albert, being a local judge, would be the one to judge the test course they jumped and sign the forms. I felt bad for being so suspicious. After about a half hour, Mrs. Albert left.

With the coast clear, I headed to the jumping arena, feeling the challenge might pull me out of my growing depression. Exercise would get my endorphins running and I'd feel better. I jumped the pasture fence, galloped across the field and let myself out the gate. With plenty of daylight left, I walked the jumping course, looking at each jump.

I had no idea what I was looking at as far as to what their proper names were, but I inspected each one. While doing so, I made mental calculations as to how to deal with each obstacle, as to the needed speed of approach, and how high I had to jump to safely make it over.

After all, math and science were my things. To me, the worst jump was now the only permanent one of the groups. It was a rail fence presently set at a yard high in the middle of a shallow in ground rectangular pool about twelve feet long and a foot deep.

I also had to figure out how many strides I had between each jump if I decided to tackle the whole course. It all gave me greater respect for anyone in this sport and a better understanding of how much it meant to my sister who had spent years working with Gold Coast towards bigger and better championships that headed her towards her Olympic dreams.

I figured it best I try one jump at a time rather than try to run the whole course at once. The first was a simple rail jump of about four feet or so that I took with ease. I walked over to the next, a fake stone wall of four feet in height made of light wood blocks painted to look like stone. I backed up to the first jump to give myself enough of a starting run, took off at a gallop, and got over the wall just fine.

There were a series of three rail jumps of four feet set close together with two strides between them. I got over all of them without touching the top rail. The fourth was a fake hedge of four feet. I got over that fine. The fifth was that horrible water hazard and I just barely got over it.

The sixth was a fake brick wall, also set at four feet. That was not bad and I made it. The next was another rail fence, that was a piece of cake. The last was the double rail fence of two different heights where Gold Coast injured himself. I made it over that one.

As I stopped to catch my breath, quite proud of myself for not falling or knocking over a fence, I was startled by clapping and turned to see Ann had been watching me by the gate. I had no idea how long she had been standing there; my concentration being riveted on the jumps.

"I knew you were good at this when I saw you jump the pasture fence this morning. Now try the whole course in a single run at a canter like in a competition. And don't knock anything down. In competition that would be four faults, and they'd take seconds off your time for the course when you finish."

"I don't know. There's no need since I have probably already had enough exercise for the day," I returned lamely.

"Chicken?"

"No. I told you. Just a trial run for today is enough. Don't want to overdo it. Remember, I'm still getting used to the new me." I knew she was trying to bait me.

"Think you can't beat a real horse and rider even with your genius brain?" she shot back, leaning over the gate.

"Don't start!" I warned. I had never walked away from a challenge in my life, though most had been mental rather than physical. She was trying to shred what little pride I had left.

She answered by making chicken clucking calls and it about drove me crazy.

"Oh, all right, just one run!" I yelled and walked up to a good starting point for the first jump, feeling my cheeks burn. "If I fall and break a leg, it's your fault."

She stuck her tongue out at me like a little kid. The arena lights flashed on a second later, as if on cue. Well, I took off at a canter and by some miracle made it over the whole eight jump course without knocking anything down.

And then I trotted over to her at the gate. She was clapping and grinning like a Cheshire cat with Aunt Bonnie right behind her holding a large plastic bag and a liter bottle of Dr. Pepper.

"I thought you could do it," Ann said.

"That was excellent. Here's your dinner. Chinese." Aunt Bonnie passed it over to me. "No time to cook. I got caught up in the first chapter of my next novel and digging around in the attic for that trunk. Found it and will start going through the game modules later."

"Thanks," I said, and slung the bag handles over my left arm to hang in the crook of my elbow, opened the soda and drank half of it. I was so thirsty. "See you tomorrow maybe, Ann."

I put the cap back on the soda and opened the arena gate with Ann still hanging on it, snickering and taking a ride with her feet on the bottom rail. I headed for the pasture gate in the early twilight. I could not help wondering what was really going on in Ann's mind and figured I'd find out sooner or later.

Possibly tomorrow, I thought.

A surprise was waiting for me in the bottom of the Chinese restaurant bag. My iPhone with a note rubber banded around it from Ann and Aunt Bonnie.

It said simply:

***Ann snatched this from your bedroom. It fits the charger in the barn office. Your mom will probably find out soon. Go and call or text your friends. If you feel comfortable, arrange to meet them in the barn on Wednesday for our games and come a little late so I can have time to talk to them about your change. Might be better this way* – Aunt Bonnie.**

Ann's message on the bottom was merely:

"Our parents are going to kill me. More later. Ann."

I tried to get ahold of both Ben and Alice, but neither answered. I figured they went to the movies or something, so I left a simple text – "I am alive and a little different. I won't see or contact you until Wednesday at Aunt Bonnie's. Don't call my house under any circumstances. You'll understand more Wednesday. Jerry."

7
Chiron's Pride

After a breakfast of a bunch of pancakes and sausage with Aunt Bonnie, I spent Sunday morning just lounging around near the spring fed brook. The water was great through the filter straw. I did more exploring the woods and watched twin fawns being born. It gave me hope. I don't know why.

I was clear on the other side of the woods doing some bird watching near home by noon when I heard Aunt Bonnie's Gator. I headed for the pasture fence. By the time I got there, I found only a plastic bag hanging on the fence post with three sub sandwiches and a liter of soda in it with a note.

Jerry, come to the barn at three. Very important you meet someone. Don't be afraid.

– Aunt Bonnie

That was very cryptic. In fact, it bugged the hell out of me. After I finished lunch, I went up to my observation point with my binoculars and got into spy mode. My suspicions of what Ann was up to hit like a bucket of cold water when I saw Mrs. Albert drive up about 2:30 P.M.

Aunt Bonnie and Ann came out of the house to meet her, and they went into the barn. I felt very betrayed by both Ann and Aunt Bonnie at that point and felt my face go hot with outrage. But the note said don't be afraid.

Perhaps Aunt Bonnie found out more information on the stone. I did not know much about Mrs. Albert except for her involvement in horse shows with my sister. Maybe there was a lot more about her. Curiosity overwhelmed me. I headed for the barn.

I heard them talking as I quietly approached the open door from the side, out of sight.

"He will be upset, but it should not last," Aunt Bonnie said. "He has a good head on his shoulders. He is a genius, in fact. And feels horrible about what happened to Gold Coast. Ann, you were no help last night. What happened to him regarding that stone, I am still trying to figure out."

"Well, I will help where I can. You know that. I'll ask my brother over at the university about any Greek legends involving stones, him being one of the anthropology professors. And the short video off Ann's iPhone is just . . . phenomenal. Jerry has a natural ability no matter what," Mrs. Albert returned.

That did it. I stepped into the doorway. "Your brother is an expert in Greek mythology, Mrs. Albert?"

When I walked into the barn, they all turned to face me, startled. Mrs. Albert's eyes widened and her mouth dropped open. She looked at me as if she had suddenly discovered a treasure rather than a monster.

"Oh my God! Phenomenal! I would not believe this in a million years, even with the video," she breathed. She took a tentative step towards me. "May I look closer? I won't do anything to embarrass you, I promise. I just want a closer look to check your physical condition."

I nodded, not happy, but figured she would not be the first one, especially if this whole ordeal ended up going public. And that is exactly where this seemed to be going. "I just hope we can figure out how to reverse this. I can't go on like this forever."

First, she lifted my t-shirt slightly and checked where my human body connected with the horse part where the neck would have been on a horse. She checked the horse part, especially my legs and hooves all around. When she finished, she stepped back and just took me in with her eyes.

"You are in your prime as a young stallion, probably of an eastern hot-blooded breed like the Arabian. Well-muscled, athletic . . . just what a jumper should be, though a little short at just under sixteen hands. However, it is not size that matters in this sport. It's heart."

"And this all means?" I came back, glaring at Ann.

She avoided my eyes. "Well, I thought . . ."

“You want me to replace Gold Coast! That is as plain as day, Ann. And you’ll keep me on a guilt trip until I do. It’s not my fault what happened to Gold Coast. I ran away because of what happened to me. Do you realize if this really goes public the media will pick it up and the government might want to take me away for all kinds of experiments? Does anyone here realize that fact?”

“Jerry . . .” Aunt Bonnie said. “You’re not being fair . . .”

“And I trusted you, Aunt Bonnie . . .” I was on the verge of a complete meltdown.

“Jerry, I understand, but you must understand you have people who care and are trying to help you cope. Not everyone is going to see you as a freak or monster.” Aunt Bonnie came over and I let her hug me. “Get a hold of yourself. Think. People love horses and centaurs have appeared in movies and books as the good guys.”

“Besides, the horse show is not televised in the big mainstream media; just local and maybe RIDE TV, which is only a horse sports channel that only horse people watch. We could be great together. Essentially, what pole vaulting, high jump, and hurdles are to track and field in high school and college jumping is to equestrian sports.

“The object for the jumper is to negotiate a series of obstacles where emphasis is placed on height and width, and to do so without lowering the height or refusing to jump any of the obstacles. The time taken to complete the course is also a factor.

"The jumping course tests a horse's athleticism, agility, and tractability while simultaneously testing a rider's precision, accuracy, and responsiveness. Perhaps most importantly, jumping tests the partnership between horse and rider. We can do this with your genius brain figuring out all the angles and velocity and my equestrian skills. We got this. Please, just stop your rant and think!" Ann begged.

"That's just plain crazy. I'm not a horse. I'm a centaur. Any reporters there will go nuts and everyone carries phones that make videos. It's at the Kentucky Horse Park; a big tourist site. Secret's out as soon as I set foot in the arena or even at their stables. Give me a freaking break."

"There are other things to think about. The hope you will give to all kids and adults who are different, be it mental capacity or physical and of course you're helping your sister towards her dream," Aunt Bonnie argued "Meanwhile, we research how to solve this mystery and get you back."

That brought me up short. "And if I say yes?"

"We have a lot of work to do and little time to do it," Mrs. Albert said. "And you may not like some of it."

"Like what?" I had to know.

"Well, I don't want to hurt your feelings, but since you are considered mostly a horse physically, to be allowed in the show you will need to be immunized against all equine diseases. And have a Coggins blood test for equine infectious anemia and one for equine piroplasmosis, a tick born disease. All horses must have health certification stating they are clear of these diseases for shows in every state. Add to that you have to be micro chipped as per new regulations.

"Then we must pick your equine name for show registration, and get certification as a show jumper through a competency test. I can take care of the show jumper certification, but we need a vet for the rest. And you must train and train hard with Ann as your rider for the next five weeks before and after your jumping test. That test needs to be done as soon as possible to get you in as the substitute for Gold Coast."

I did a face palm. "Vet? Oh my God! What shots?"

"Rabies, tetanus, Eastern, and Western encephalomyelitis, rhinopneumonitis, Influenza, rhino-flu combination, strangles, and Potomac horse fever." Mrs. Albert counted them off on her fingers. "And the Coggins, piroplasmosis blood tests, and don't forget the microchip."

I put both my hands on my face in a double face palm. I looked at them between my fingers. "And who can we trust to do that?"

"I can get Dr. Pratt. He is trustworthy. I went to high school when he was a senior and even dated him a few times," Mrs. Albert said, her cheeks turning a bit red.

"I already had a tetanus shot. Won't this immunization affect my human part? Logically my blood is going to come up really weird," I went on, and took my hands off my face and folded my arms across my chest.

"I'm sure Dr. Pratt will understand the weirdness part," Aunt Bonnie said. "Only possible problem is the samples have to go to the state vet at the Agricultural Department. But they will be looking only for Coggins and piroplasmosis evidence."

I looked over at Gold Coast's stall. He had his head over the door and was staring at me. I looked from him to Ann, Aunt Bonnie, and Mrs. Albert and back to him.

Mrs. Albert spoke up at that moment. "Jerry, let me explain things in greater detail so you understand a little more. I know the equestrian world is basically foreign to you. Riding on the US Equestrian Team in the Olympics requires four things: total dedication, the right horse or horses, the right coach, training experience, and money. By total dedication, I mean a candidate needs to be someone who spends practically every waking moment at the barn, riding and working with as many different horses as they possibly can when they aren't in school."

"I sure fit the different classification," I cracked, trying to relieve my anger.

Mrs. Albert smiled and went on. "Total dedication also means that they spend hours riding and training every day, all summer long, regardless of the weather. It means they spend hours doing grunt work like cleaning stalls, grooming horses, feeding, and so forth. They need to be around when horses are sick, and around when mares foal.

"They need to have the experience of holding the lead rope while the veterinarian puts down an old, tired, and often seriously ill or injured equine friend. When they've had experiences like that, and had years of them, they may stand a chance of becoming a USET member. Being dedicated means giving up their social life so they can train and prepare for the top-level A and AA circuit shows and the selection trials that will follow.

"For Ann it could mean being tutored on the road, and having to do her homework in a tent on the show grounds so that she can still get a college education while she is pursuing her sport. It means spending months on the road every year, going from one show to another. But most of all, it means she has to win, and win a lot, so she will stand a chance of attracting the attention of the team selectors.

"And your mom and dad know this and are planning for it, starting with the choice of college with equine programs. Most of what prize money she has won in the bigger shows is going toward her equine education."

"I thought so. I just have not paid all that much attention to the details since it is not exactly my world. I guess you are right. I needed to learn more facts about the process."

"Now's a good a time as ever," Ann said, pulling an old burr out of my tail.

Mrs. Albert nodded. "I can certainly help there. Most people who want to be Olympic caliber riders plan their careers, Jerry. They also start out riding ponies as very young children, in most cases like your sister and I did."

"You are an Olympic rider?" I burst out.

"Not yet, but I am in the running." A smile ran across her face. "And as your parents know, let me mention that equestrian sports aren't cheap. Horses are expensive to buy and keep, and equestrian sports are the most expensive ones in the Olympics. Most riders on that level have to have sponsors because there is no way they could ever pay all the costs involved on their own.

"Also essential are good coaching and training to anybody who wants to ride at the international level. It takes years of experience to learn to ride well enough to get accepted onto any international team. That's the reason why you will never see children or young teenagers riding in the Olympics, Jerry.

"Simply taking one or two lessons a week and jaunting around for pleasure the rest of the time will never get you on a team. You have to work for that honor, and work damned hard. Most of the current team members are professionals who've been in this business their whole lives. Some of them are in their fifties and sixties, in fact, because it takes that long to reach the level they are at in competing."

"In the end how are riders selected?" I asked, curiously.

"Teams are typically chosen by computer rankings that are based on the amount of money a rider and horse have earned in a given season or pair of seasons. This happens after a larger pool of riders is chosen by the selectors in the different disciplines. The selectors are professionals themselves, and many are former Olympians. That initial large pool is referred to as the 'long list' which I am on.

"From it, the riders who will compete in events like the Olympics are chosen based on their competitive records. Those who have won more stand a greater likelihood of being picked for what is called the 'short list' than those who haven't won as much. The 'short list' is the group of eight or so riders from which the final team will be chosen. Since teams are normally made up of four riders, their horses, and two alternates, the minimum short list must be number eight.

"This procedure I just outlined is used in all three of the Olympic equestrian disciplines, not just show jumping alone. Ann has a long way to go, but she has a strong start with all her past and recent winnings with Gold Coast. It is just very unfortunate what happened to Gold Coast at this time. Your parents cannot afford another trained jumper to replace him and even if they could, there is too little time to get one adapted to your sister for this season."

All that I heard from Mrs. Albert about this whole Olympic thing hit like a cold tide, filling in all questions with crystal clarity and cooled my outrage. I knew more than ever how much a career in equine sports meant to Ann. She had planned her whole life to become part of the US Equestrian Team.

She was damn good at what she did. Her room was stuffed with trophies. To miss out on a summer of events would be catastrophic. Me? I had no real plans except maybe go to MIT or Berkeley. That would not happen for a year. My career path was aimed at ending up in some branch of scientific research, preferably cosmology or in a think tank.

I had nothing that was immediately threatened, really. And if we did not find a way to change me back; then what? Centaurs don't go to MIT to study dark matter and string theory. I sighed. Everyone was looking at me expectantly.

"Oh, okay. But if this blows up in our faces, it is not my fault," I said.

Ann was hugging me around my human body as far up as she could reach before I could take a breath.

"We have a lot of work to do and now's a good time to start. Let's see if Gold Coast's saddle fits you after a good brushing," Mrs. Albert said matter-of-factly.

Well, I was soon standing in front of three women staring at me in a jumping saddle with breast collar to keep it from slipping back, hoof boots since I did not wear shoes, splint boot leg protectors, and bell boots on my front hooves. Then Aunt Bonnie dashed to the tack room again and came out with a riding helmet she put on my head.

"Can't forget that," she said cheerily.

I felt like a gladiator or something and was not happy at all. "You expect me to be able to jump with all this on and Ann on my back?" I complained.

"You will get used to it. It is all safety equipment required by the USEF," Mrs. Albert stated.

"We still have to come up with some kind of replacement for reins so I can balance right and give any needed signals, and before you bitch and moan, Jerry, I don't mean a bridle." Ann gave me a light smack on the butt.

I turned my human torso to look at her and frowned. "No whips, no crops, or spurs or it's off . . . no go. I'm not a horse. I'm a centaur."

"Spurs are optional according to the rules and I won't wear them in your case since with your genius brain you're going to pick this all up really quick," Ann shot back.

"Good."

"I think I might have something that might work." Aunt Bonnie tapped her chin thoughtfully. "My husband's old deer stand safety harness. We can take the leg straps off and rig the chest straps so you can cross the reins over his chest for any emergency signals, and they will be at the right height for reins. Plus, it will keep the purists from bitching about no bridle."

"Great idea, Bonnie!" Mrs. Albert nodded.

She went right off to get it out of the garage. In no time, they had it all finished and me standing there trussed up like a turkey.

"Now for the experiment," Mrs. Albert announced. "Let's go to the jump arena and you go over one jump after a trot around the ring to warm up with Ann in the saddle."

"This ought to be good for a laugh," I said in a snarky tone as I walked with them to the jump arena, glad the sun was dipping down, and no one could see us from the road.

Under the arena lights, wearing all the tack and having a weight on my back that was my sister were the most bizarre sensations I ever had in my life. I was afraid I'd lose her over the jump, but her leg pressure let me know she was not going to budge.

"This is just as strange for me as it is you," Ann said. "Shrinks would have a field day."

"Yeah, don't I know that," I returned, and broke into a trot.

Around we went with Mrs. Albert and Aunt Bonnie watching our every move. I quickly found all that equipment was no bother at all; probably no more of a problem than all that football padding Andrew and his Neanderthals wore. Soon the rail jump loomed ahead.

"Hang on," I said to Ann.

I changed to a slow canter in my approach when she lightly put her heel on my horse ribs and over we went. I felt her lean over my human back the same way she would over Gold Coast's neck. I kept my arms close to my body the best I could. We landed smoothly. Aunt Bonnie clapped.

"Very good, both of you. We'll try the rest of the course tomorrow," Mrs. Albert called as I turned to head back to the gate where we met them. She patted my horse shoulder. "Now we've got to come up with a name for you as a horse for registration."

"How about Chiron's Pride?" Aunt Bonnie grinned. "Keep the Ancient Greek theme."

"Makes sense to me." I grinned back. "I rather like it."

"Clever," Mrs. Albert returned.

As soon as they helped me out of the tack, Aunt Bonnie called in a big order of pizza. Mrs. Albert headed home before it arrived. Mom and Dad came over to eat with us, and as usual, we shared our day. All of us agreed not to bring any more people into our family secret than we had to at this point. When our barn pizza party was over, I headed out to the pasture gate.

Aunt Bonnie called after me. "Don't forget to stay in the woods tomorrow morning while the gate is being installed. I'll be down with your breakfast before they get here."

I waved, closed the pasture gate behind me, and trotted toward the woods, jumping the fence easily. I could not help feeling things were about to get a lot stranger on this new path.

8
The Impossible Patient and Geek Squad Reunited

Mom came down to the pasture fence with Aunt Bonnie to share a great breakfast of sausage and scrambled eggs on Monday just before Joe was due to arrive to put in the pasture gate.

"Since the barn office has Wi-Fi, you can finish your classes in the stall you've been using. I'm arranging for home schooling by computer today once I open my office. I gave Aunt Bonnie your laptop. Leave it in the barn office on its charger when you are finished and don't message your friends on Facebook. It's already bad enough you will be discovered by thousands of people once that horse show comes around, but I hope we will have an answer by then as to how to reverse whatever caused all this."

Aunt Bonnie immediately winked at me and Mom did not catch it. "Until we resolve this whole issue, I'm not renting out that box stall and I've asked the five other renters to call before coming so I can make sure the barn is unlocked for them. I made up the excuse suspicious characters are in the area that are robbery suspects, and I had to remove our hidden emergency key. It's sort of a white lie. However, the Greenes' had their tractor stolen two days ago. Only Ann and Mrs. Albert can come and go as they please since all of you have work to do and they are the only ones that have keys."

"Thanks," I said, quite glad one big worry was over. "What about exams?"

"You can take them over the internet, too," Mom replied.

"Yes! No more Andrew Collins and his Neanderthals for the rest of the school year!" I shouted, and reared boisterously, forgetting myself and startled both Mom and Aunt Bonnie into almost dropping their plates. "Sorry."

Mom smiled. "At least he will be gone in your senior year. Now I better get on to the office. I have a 9 a.m. closing to get to, and then calls to make to the school board."

"Joe will be here in about twenty minutes. Jerry, keep out of sight until he's gone. I'll bring lunch later," Aunt Bonnie said. They both packed up the basket and drove away in the Gator.

Bored, I spent the morning well hidden in the woods watching Joe and another guy put on the new gate that would allow easier access to the woods. He finished before noon, which was great timing. Aunt Bonnie brought a family bucket of KFC chicken, coleslaw, and mashed potatoes and something else; that *D & D* module she had been searching for the last day or so.

"Well, I finally found it and read through it and it may help us in our search. The module story takes place in a cave system under the ruins of a Greek temple, and among the jewels that the party of adventurers turn up in their quest is the Circe's Stone of Change," she said, and handed me the module booklet.

As I flipped through it while I ate, she continued. "The stone is a moonstone, and Circe is said to have used it to turn men into beasts by putting it in wine and chanting a spell over it before she had servant girls give it to them at a banquet.

"And the author of this module is none other than Mrs. Albert's brother, Dr. Alexander Grant, in the anthropology department at the university. I talked to her last night when she called with the very same info and told me when he was in college, he wrote a few *D&D* game modules to earn extra money with his free-lance writing that helped pay his college bills."

"Wow, so we are right on thinking it is cursed," I said. "We have to find a way of breaking the curse. But more questions come to mind like, how did it get here? And is anyone looking for it?"

"That may take a while to solve, unfortunately," she sighed before biting into a crunchy drumstick. "Maybe we can all put our heads together at the game on Wednesday evening after we reintroduce you to your friends and swear them to secrecy."

"Don't tell Mom about our plan."

"Never fear. And don't you forget you have jumping lessons after Ann gets back from school today and walks Gold Coast for a little exercise. Mrs. Albert will be here, too."

"I won't forget."

"Oh, and you will be staying overnight in the barn. Dr. Pratt is coming tomorrow at 10 a.m. Mrs. Albert will be having breakfast with us before he arrives and staying on to help ease him into our new *Twilight Zone* reality."

"I just hope he stays quiet about it and the state does not notice anything abnormal in my blood," I said, hating having yet another worry to chew on. "Not looking forward to becoming a pin cushion, either."

The afternoon passed quickly, and soon I saw Ann walking along Gold Coast. Mrs. Albert arrived shortly after Ann returned him to his stall. I used the new pasture gate and trotted down to the barn to get all tacked up and ready for some jumps.

I didn't get a chance to talk to Mrs. Albert at all about her brother. Everything was horse business. I knocked two rails off two jumps in our practice run of the full course because of bad timing, and the fact they moved a few of the jumps around to a different configuration. The rails were not hit hard.

In fact, I hardly grazed them with my hoof boots, but a slight touch was all it took. I was not happy with my run, being a perfectionist and all. We ran the course two more times, and my best run was the last one. At least I got a nice cool down walk, warm sponge bath, and rub down after practice. Eat your hearts out football jocks. All you get is a shower in the high school stinky locker room.

Dinner was a huge grilled chicken salad. I slept better that night than I had in a long time. In fact, I totally zonked out as soon as I closed my eyes and stayed asleep until I heard the barn door open and Aunt Bonnie enter for her morning chores.

Not long afterwards, she let the five boarders and Drama Queen out to the pasture for the first time that spring and went back to the kitchen to make breakfast. Mrs. Albert came into the barn when Aunt Bonnie returned with her picnic basket full of pancakes, sausage, and a thermos of coffee.

The first thing I said to Mrs. Albert was, "Thanks for helping with the stone mystery."

"You're welcome. I just wish it could have been more. I'm wondering where it came from and how long the effect will be. But regardless, it is very kind of you to help your sister in her quest to reach the Olympics. Not everyone would be willing to do that for a sibling if they were in the same circumstance."

"I hope this does not happen to anyone else, and that we find a solution." I stuffed my mouth with pancake dripping in honey. Soon as I swallowed, I changed the subject. "What worries me right now is Dr. Pratt."

"I think he'll be fine with it," Aunt Bonnie said.

"I think he will about have a heart attack," I came back.

"He's seen a lot of strange things in his career," Mrs. Albert added.

"Well, I'm not exactly a two-headed calf," I remarked, and finished my last sausage and handed Aunt Bonnie my empty plate.

Mrs. Albert laughed. "No, you are not, but I think he will be fine."

Aunt Bonnie gathered up the dishes and headed back to the house to drop them off while Mrs. Albert gave me a quick brushing to get rid of stable dust and the bits of bedding that stuck to me. Soon we heard Dr. Pratt's van driving up outside. The ladies left me and closed the barn door behind them. I went over to listen through it.

I heard the van door open and close and Dr. Pratt's cheery, "Good morning, ladies. I trust our patient is ready. It's great that Ann found a replacement so quickly."

Mrs. Albert's voice was next. "John, I want you to look at this video. It is important for you to see this before you step into the barn. It is not a joke or hoax. None of us have the tech skills or equipment to pull that kind of thing off. This is your patient. We'll understand if you refuse. We only ask you not breathe a word of it to anyone."

"Sorry to say this, but no one will believe you if you do mention it," Aunt Bonnie's voice sounded.

There was a long silence.

"Oh, my God! You are kidding me . . . really? Is that . . . Oh, my God, it's Jerry! How?" Dr. Pratt rambled on.

"We are trying to solve the mystery. But meanwhile, he has promised his sister he'd stand in for Gold Coast. He's all horse where it counts. We need a clean bill of health to do this. If everything is legal, no one can object since he is mostly horse. I know this all sounds crazy. It's like living in the *Twilight Zone*."

"But is he okay . . . I mean his mind. And a big worry is once this goes public with the horse show and all, every nutcase in the crypto zoology field and government will be asking for him if not outright find a way to legally, or illegally, get a hold of him," Dr. Pratt went on.

"He is still Jerry, I assure you," Aunt Bonnie said. "There is just more of him that happens to be a horse."

The second the door started to open, I backed away. Dr. Pratt stood there staring in awe, his eyes wide.

"Hi, Dr. Pratt," I said lamely, and gave him a little wave and an idiot grin.

He tightened his grip on his bag as he approached me slowly, holding out his right hand. I let him put it on my horse shoulder.

"Unbelievable." All he could say as he stepped back and looked at me from front to rump in a slow, critical manner. "Do you feel all right?"

"So far. I just want my old self back. But meanwhile, I'm helping my sister. She can't afford to miss a season of events. I know it's risky, and I'm probably the biggest idiot to risk everything." I still felt like a total idiot for agreeing to it.

"You know this is highly irregular. You are still part human, and I can't guarantee the vaccines will not affect you in an adverse way," he warned. "The blood tests may show up strange and start an investigation by the Department of Agriculture."

"But the bigger part of me is a horse and needs the shots for health reasons and so I can compete if I'm allowed. I doubt very much that the DA will be doing a genetic test. From biology class I learned blood cells look pretty much the same in higher animals, including humans," I replied.

"True," he agreed, putting his bag on a bale of bedding and opening it.

The exam was extensive. I did not particularly like a thermometer stuck up my butt or him fingering my family jewels. He took blood from both my human and horse body for good measure, and I felt like a pin cushion by the time the vaccines were done.

The worst thing was the microchip that was injected by a big bore needle at my horse shoulder where it joined my human body. The pain made me cuss loud enough to probably be heard in the next county.

"The verdict on his present condition?" Aunt Bonnie asked as soon as Dr. Pratt was finished.

"Not being an expert in centaur anatomy, mind you, I'd say both parts are perfectly healthy, with the strangest cardiovascular and respiratory systems I have ever seen. If he starts running a fever or shows signs of a rash, call me. Now, while I'm here I'll take a look at Gold Coast."

Gold Coast was doing as well as expected and Dr. Pratt left promising to get the health papers to us as soon as the report came back in a week or so, and promised to keep our secret at the risk of being called ready for the rubber room. The next big confrontation with my real world would be my Wednesday night game with Alice and Ben.

I spent the rest of the morning and part of the afternoon happily on the computer with my home schooling in the barn. It was a welcome part of my old life put back in place. Late afternoon was taken up by jumping practice after Ann walked Gold Coast around the barn a few times and let him nibble a bit of the new spring grass.

Jumping practice went well despite Mrs. Albert having us mostly work on our timing over that combination jump with only two strides between three rail fences and dropped that to one stride between the fences. There were times Ann and I fought each other for control, which almost resulted in disaster.

I did not develop a fever or rash and slept like I was in a coma. Wednesday was once again spent on home schooling and later more jumping practice. Needless to say, I was counting the hours until game time and was a bit annoyed at Dad deciding it was warm enough to grill hamburgers on our back patio.

He thought it was good getting together as a family, including Aunt Bonnie, for dinner out on our patio in weather more like early summer. I ate a dozen hamburgers, a whole serving bowl of salad, and a bag of fries.

After dinner I went back to Aunt Bonnie's place to help her get the boarders back into the barn for the night and get ready for the games. After the horses were all in their stalls, we set the game up on an old sheet of plywood balanced on two sawhorses in the middle of the aisle with room to spare.

The dungeon map was tacked to it, and Aunt Bonnie put the Dungeon Master's screen up with her bag of dice behind it sitting on our module book. I went to my stall to wait.

I heard everyone approach in the dark and saw a flashlight beam under the closed barn door.

"You both have got to stay cool," Aunt Bonnie said.

"We know something is different," Alice stated.

"He texted us the other day to let us know he is okay. But we heard nothing more from him," Ben added.

"He said not to call his house," Alice finished Ben's thought.

"Well, there is a reason. His parents do not want to have it spread around what happened and do not want him contacting you fearing you could not keep the secret. And without further suspense." Aunt Bonnie shoved open the barn door.

"Hi, guys," I called, waving from the stall.

"What's the big deal? And what are you doing in there, man?" Ben demanded.

"Just come in and stay on that side of our table," I returned.

"This is just plain silly," Alice complained, her face dark with a frown.

They all walked in and Aunt Bonnie closed the door behind them. I pushed my stall door open and walked into the aisle. "It's Andrew Collins' fault. You heard him call me a horse's ass, and now I have one. That stone I had is cursed."

They stood there open-mouthed and dropped their gaming folders.

"Oh, my God!" Alice breathed, and stared as her right hand slowly covered her open mouth.

"Awesome!" Ben burst out. "You'd be the biggest hit of the century at the next Comic-Con."

They both rushed me and we had a group hug, not wanting to let go, or at least it felt that way.

"This news does not go beyond this barn. Do I make myself clear?" Aunt Bonnie broke in.

They both looked at her crestfallen.

"I can't risk it getting out yet," I said. "It's bad enough this will eventually get out to the public at that Cross-County Hunt Horse Show in June. I'm standing in for Ann's injured horse."

"Are you crazy?" Alice burst out, lightly slapping my horse shoulder. "That's just asking to get kidnapped by a government lab or some nutcase crypto zoologist. You're a bigger story than Big Foot or a UFO landing!"

"We are hoping to have this curse broken by then, or shortly after. We found the stone and I put it in a safe place," Aunt Bonnie went on. "Near as we can tell through some research is that the stone is what Circe used to turn men into beasts."

"Holy shit, man. Greek myths are real?" Ben blurted. "Awesome!"

"My theory is they exist in another dimension. Think Multiverse instead of Universe. The different dimensions touch sometimes, like soap bubbles and portals are formed. I also think someone may have stolen it and dropped it in our dimension. We just happened to stumble upon it. Aunt Bonnie and I tried to reverse it. I held it, wished to be back to my original self, and got my hand shocked and burned for the effort." I showed them my hand that still had a red spot.

Alice grabbed it for a closer look. "You, okay?"

"It still hurts, but I'm fine." I shrugged. "Maybe between all of us, we can come up with a way to correct this mess."

"Until then, are you all ready to continue our game?" Aunt Bonnie asked.

We all looked at each other, grinned and said in unison. "Yes."

It was great to have our Geek Squad back together. It made my day feel a lot more like my normal life. I could feel the bulk of my depression melt like butter in a frying pan.

We got out our papers and dice and Aunt Bonnie rolled up a wandering monster behind her screen. It was a particularly nasty creature called a Roper, a shapeshifter that looked like a stalagmite or part of a cave floor, had a wide toothy mouth, and six sticky thick rope-like excretions to snag victims.

We were so busy combating the Roper that none of us noticed we were being watched in the real world until what sounded like a bucket being tipped over outside hit the barn siding by a high window in a boarder's stall. By the time we all ran out to investigate, whoever it was had disappeared into the night. A wooden apple crate was right at the side of the barn under the window, and the bucket was on its side right next to it.

"This bucket belongs by the pump. Someone moved it. If you don't mind, Jerry, I'd like you to sleep in the locked barn tonight." Aunt Bonnie said when she picked up the bucket.

"Fine with me," I returned.

"And I think I'll be putting another security light or two up around here. Maybe add a camera," she added.

Then we went back into the barn to continue our game.

9
The Gift and Mepos

The next morning, I had just finished a pre-exam quiz in college level physics at around ten when Aunt Bonnie came into the barn and over to my stall. She looked a bit annoyed.

"Sorry, Jerry, but I've got to have you go back to your hut. One of the boarders, Miss Evans who owns Diamond in the stall across the aisle from you, is meeting the farrier here at eleven. I hope I didn't disturb you from something important, did I?"

"No. Just finished up a physics pre finals quiz," I said, logged out of my laptop I had balanced on the stall door sill, closed it, and handed it to her.

"I'll put it on the charger in the office and give you your iPhone so we can keep in touch. Especially if you see anyone suspicious hanging around in our woods. Don't need my tractor or Gator stolen. I'll bring down your lunch as soon as I can."

I opened the stall door and followed her to the office. She handed me the iPhone, and I headed for the pasture. As I approached the new gate to the woods at a quick trot, I got the creepy feeling I was being watched.

You know, that hair-on-the-back-of-your-neck-sticking-up chill?

I could not shake it and slowed to a cautious walk, looking around at the shadows in the spring green underbrush along the tree line. The warm weather had everything growing fast. I did not spot anything out of place but remained cautious as I let myself through the new gate and headed down the deer trail at a walk alert to the slightest turn of a leaf.

As I walked past a tall elderberry bush with my hut in view, the sudden sight of a bow and quiver of arrows leaning against the hut right by the entry brought me up short. I instantly backed behind the bush and peeked through the new foliage.

I noticed it was by no means a modern bow. It was a composite recurve bow of ancient design. The quiver appeared to be made of leather and also of ancient design of exquisite quality.

I stood, listening and watching the forest around me for a long time. Not finding another presence, I crept up on the hut and peeked in. All was as I had left it. On closer visual inspection of the bow and arrows, I identified them as from Ancient Greece, but they looked and felt new. A big thank you for that ability goes to weapons illustrations in *Dungeons and Dragons* and my paying attention in Ancient History class to the painted pottery of the time.

The bowstring was on, but unstrung. Though I was far from the athletic type in my human part, the bow appeared to have been made to fit me, which was kind of a scary thought that started a bunch of questions flying through my mind. Where did it come from? Who brought it? Did it have to do with the prowler last night? Was it all connected to the stone?

I put my iPhone in my shirt bag in the hut and then picked up the bow to figure out how to string it. I certainly knew the physics of it, the conversion of potential energy to kinetic energy. However, stringing it was a bit problematic.

Sure, I placed the strung end against the ground as I had seen in the movies, but bending the other end down to slip on the bowstring was not easy. It was like trying to string Odysseus' bow in the Ancient Greek myth. I did not seem to have the upper body strength needed and that frustrated me. Even though I stopped my effort, it still felt like I was being watched and that embarrassed me, adding to my sour mood.

Out of sheer aggravation I yelled out, "I'm a centaur, damn it! I should be able to do this!"

I made a final strained effort, feeling my arm muscles burn, and got the bowstring in place more by a force of will. I sighed deeply out of relief and just stared at the bow in my hands.

I had to let Aunt Bonnie know immediately. Things were turning just too strange. I leaned the bow against the hut as I went in, grabbed my iPhone, and punched in her number.

"Jerry." Her voice was low and strained. "Can I call you back?"

"Aunt Bonnie, I don't know what's going on, but I found a bow and quiver of arrows at my hut," I blurted. "You've got to come down here and look."

"The farrier's here and so is Miss Evans. I'll be over when I can break away from here. See you in a bit."

There was dead air.

I put the phone back in my shirt bag and returned outside. When I glanced out into the woods, I saw something round hanging in one of the trees about five feet off the ground and fifty yards out. A mix of curiosity and dread drove me to investigate.

I cautiously approached it and about halfway to it, I realized it was a target. When I reached it, I found it was made of rough leather stitched together with sinew, stuffed with grass, and had a bullseye painted on it in white paint.

"This is getting way too much like the *Twilight Zone*," I half mumbled to myself and turned back toward my hut, noting every branch that would have been the slightest obstacle to a clear shot had been broken off all the way to the hut.

On my way back, I felt a chill down both my backs. Someone was still around and watching me. I could feel it. I stopped and looked around.

"I know you are here. Show yourself!" I yelled at the woods.

Only a blue jay scolded back an answer. Something moved through the brush behind me. Startled, I swung around to look. It was only the doe with twin fawns.

"Shit," I muttered, and trotted the rest of the way back to my hut and went inside. I needed to talk to someone.

I looked at my watch. It was 11:30 a.m., and my school lunch time with Ben and Alice. I pulled out the phone and punched in Ben's number, first hoping he had his cell phone with him and not in his locker. Phone use was only allowed at lunch.

"Hey, Jerry," came his voice.

"Hey, yourself. Things are getting really strange here. An ancient Greek bow with arrows showed up at my woodland hut with a target in the woods," I said.

"You have a hut? Where?"

"Aunt Bonnie bought the thirty-five-acre woods between her place and my house. Forgot to tell you. It is sort of my safe zone, but now I'm not so sure."

"Not good. I'll let Alice know. She's got the twenty-four-hour bug. Want me to come over after school?"

"No." I suddenly thought better of it. Without Alice's mom to drop them both off, it would be a five-mile bike ride for him from his house on a thoroughbred farm where his father was the foreman on a road traveled by the Neanderthals in their pickup trucks. "I'll be okay. Just wanted you to know. Will call you as soon as Aunt Bonnie and I figure this out."

"Okay. Catch you later."

There was dead air again. I shut the phone off to save the battery and tucked it back into my shirt bag. Then I turned around to go out the doorway.

About two yards from it stood a satyr. Well, actually a faun. Satyrs were ugly dwarfs that have the ears and tail of a horse. A faun was the true half goat, half man, like the god Pan. Startled, I froze staring and breathed, "What the . . ."

I judged him to be about my age, and he was of normal human size. The human part was sun bronzed. His head was covered in curly dark brown hair from which protruded small horns of about six inches and his ears were those of a goat.

His face had sharp aquiline features with large, expressive brown eyes and had barely a peach fuzz beard. The fur covered goat half of his body was dark brown with tan under parts, he had no clothes on, and a leather bag was hung over his left shoulder on a strap.

His smile brimmed with secrets, and he said in a normal voice, "Hello. My name is Mepos."

I blinked in disbelief, which was rather funny considering my own appearance. "How do you know English?"

He shrugged. "Your world, I guess. Don't really know."

"What do you want?" I knew well their reputation from the myths of fauns and satyrs being the original party animals.

He looked at the ground as if struggling to tell the truth and poked at a stick with his right-cloven hoof. He looked at me. "I brought you what you will need."

"From where and why?" I snapped. I was tired of riddles.

"From someplace else and to help put things right."

"Your answers are about as clear as mud," I grumbled, and stepped toward him.

Mepos took a step backwards, and his eyes looked wildly about as if for an easy escape route.

"I need answers. Real answers. Quit screwing around," I shouted, and stamped my right front hoof.

"You need to learn to use that bow; to master it," he came back, and took off at a run down the deer trail that led deeper into the woods.

"You little . . ." I charged after him. "Come back here!"

He was far quicker than I expected, and I only chased him about a hundred yards before I lost him in the underbrush. I heard the Gator approaching and galloped back to the pasture gate. I reached it in time to meet Aunt Bonnie as she opened the gate.

"You won't believe what just happened!" I shouted at her as I approached.

"At this point I would not be surprised at anything," she said, and reached for the basket on the passenger seat. "Tuna fish salad sandwiches and iced tea. Hope that is okay."

"Fine." I joined her.

"Now what's all the fuss?"

"A faun by the name of Mepos showed up. Said I had to learn how to use the bow and said he showed up to put things right. Real obtuse and enigmatic answers. And I am not hallucinating. When I demanded more answers, he took off. I chased him and I lost him in the woods."

She went silent and her eyebrows knitted. "Well, that proves our theory of another dimension touching ours. There must be a portal around here somewhere."

"Just what I need. More mysteries and on top of dealing with Ann and the horse shows," I complained as I took the plate of three tuna sandwiches she handed me.

"It may be wise to master that bow. Looks to me like things may get more complicated before all this is over." She took a bite of her sandwich. "I'll go with you back to the hut to take a look at it when we finish."

We both ate quickly without further discussion and headed for the hut. Aunt Bonnie inspected the bow, holding it as if it was a treasured relic.

"This is fantastic; a beautiful piece of work." She leaned the bow against the hut and picked an arrow out of the quiver. "Wow, iron arrowhead, finely forged." Then she looked around on the ground. "Look, tracks, large goat tracks. Wish Frank was still alive. He was an excellent tracker. Never lost a deer. I bet if we follow these, we could find out where the entrance to that dimensional portal is."

"I tried to track him from where I lost him in that chase. It was a waste of time," I said.

"Well, let's try something different. Sleep out here tonight. See if he shows up. If he says he must put something right, he will be back sometime. We have to find out if it has something to do with the stone. For all we know, he could have been the one that took it and lost it here. It might be a good idea not to let him know we have it."

"Don't I know it," I came back.

"Be careful." She put the arrow back in the quiver. "He is a creature not to be trusted. Too many unknowns."

"Don't worry about that. Maybe I should get a gallon of wine. That should get him to talk."

We both had a laugh over that.

"Only as a last resort," Aunt Bonnie said, suddenly quite serious. "I'll see you later when you practice with Ann. And for God's sake, do not mention Mepos to her or anyone for that matter. Meanwhile, try out that bow and don't overdo it. It has to at least have a seventy-five-pound draw weight." She patted my horse shoulder.

"Catch you later," I called after her as she left to hike down the trail toward the pasture fence.

She waved.

I picked up the bow and looked at it. Gripping it with my left hand, I tried drawing back on the string with my right and found it not as easy as it looked.

In fact, I could hardly pull it back to my nose before my arm muscles began to shake and burn in protest, forcing me to carefully ease it back into its original position. I mumbled to myself, "This is nuts."

10
Lessons

Worry about Mepos preyed on my mind right up to jumping practice. Mrs. Albert decided it was imperative to have me learn the proper names for the jumps so we'd all be on the same page in that respect and on top of that, to have us practice the sharp turns we'd run into in the show ring.

"Jerry, the names aren't all that hard to remember, but you have to be able to jump them for both your certification test and be prepared to jump them at the show," she began as we followed her to the jump arena. "A vertical consists of poles or planks placed one directly above another on the standards with no spread, or width, to jump.

"Oxers are two verticals close together to make the jump wider, also called a spread. They come in various types. A square oxer has both top poles of an equal height. An ascending oxer has the furthest pole higher than the first. A descending oxer has the furthest pole lower than the closest. A Swedish oxer has the poles slanting in opposite directions, so that they appear to form an 'X' shape when seen head on.

"The other types include a triple bar, which is a spread fence using three elements of graduating heights. The wall jump is made to resemble a brick or stone wall, but the 'bricks' are constructed of lightweight material, and fall easily when knocked. The Hogsback has a spread fence with three rails where the tallest pole is in the center.

"The combination is usually two or three jumps in a row, with no more than two strides between each. Two jumps in a row are called double combinations, and three jumps in a row are called triple combinations and all can be tricky. The open water is a wide ditch of water and a similar one is the Liverpool, which is a ditch or large tray of water under a vertical or oxer.

"And lastly, there is the brush jump that has brush, or faux grass, on the top of it. Normally, a horse is able to see over the top of it and most of the time the horse's belly will hit the grass on top. These jumps have a cut out in the middle and brush on the side. There may be a fence or log on the bottom of the jump. The jump could be anywhere from two to five feet tall. These jumps also may be wide, causing the horse to stretch out its legs and chest."

Ann had to add, "And at the shows they will all be decorated real fancy, which will make them distracting. I have seen some horses refuse to jump them at shows. I get to walk the course and will tell you what mix they are using before we go in so you will also know. You understanding me is about the only advantage we have over the other entries."

"Horses take months to learn how to take the jumps. We have only weeks, but you also have the advantage of being part human with a genius level of intelligence. You won't refuse them like some horses do," Mrs. Albert countered, and frowned at Ann.

"Well, I can misjudge distance and speed needed. That happens all the time in human track and field," I commented, not wanting to get too complacent.

"Right now, you both have to get used to working as a team more than ever to get through that test next week, or you won't have to worry about the show. Ann, you have been through the test before, but still don't get cocky. What we've been doing so far has just been small potatoes.

"This afternoon we will practice the sharp turns they will be throwing at you in the pattern configurations at the show. You both need your full concentration on what you are doing. We will get you ready with all the proper paperwork, and we should have less of a problem with the powers that be at the USEF rejecting the idea of what is supposed to be a mythical equine being competing as a stand in horse entry for a jumping event."

It was then I noticed the jumps that could be moved had been rearranged in a new pattern out in our arena.

"You will be running this in a figure eight; first the vertical, then ascending oxer, the wall, then the combination, brush and square oxer," Mrs. Albert announced. "I'll let both of you walk around this new course first, and then do warm up exercise with a couple of trots around the arena and then take on the course."

"I don't think this is going to come off so good," I complained, finding it suddenly hard to think of anything else but Mepos and wondering if he was watching from the woods.

"You can do it. You've done it before in a different sequence," Ann said with confidence.

"Don't jinx yourself, Jerry," Mrs. Albert called cheerily after us as we started our warmup exercise.

Well, the first attempt at the new configuration of jumps had me off stride real fast thanks to the quick turns and in trying to compensate despite Ann's signals. I knocked a block off the wall and top rail off the ascending oxer and one of the triple combination jumps. It was frustrating.

We did two more runs at the full course, and the best run was still with a knock down of the ascending oxer top rail. None of us were happy with the afternoon practice. We had only a week until the test to improve.

Dinner was pizza in the barn with my family. Though I could not mention Mepos, that little mutton head was all I could think about. Everyone else but Aunt Bonnie assumed I was fretting about the jumping certification test.

Before returning to my hut, Ann had me watch a YouTube video of a previous year's Olympic Grand Prix jumping competition on my laptop for further education.

Her comment as she clicked on the video was, "This is a much bigger challenge than the show coming up. In the Grand Prix, the horse jumps a course of ten to sixteen obstacles, with heights up to five feet three inches and spreads of up to six feet seven inches. It is timed and there is a jump off to find the winner."

"Oh, piece of cake . . . not," I commented and settled in to watch about the scariest thing since I saw *Alien* when I was six.

It was hard to believe horses could jump that high and stretch the way they did over jumps that seemed almost like major construction projects gone mad. On my walk back to my hut, I was afraid the video would give me nightmares.

I settled down in my bedding under the quilt, my mind racing over what I had seen and trying to think of something else. I hate it when my mind will not let me fall to sleep quickly. In the light of the waning moon, my eyes fell on the bow and quiver I had hung inside the hut on pegs made from branches stuck through the wall. I sighed and closed my eyes. I drifted toward sleep.

"You should not keep a bow strung like that," Mepos's voice broke through the quiet.

It shocked me into immediate wakefulness as if I had bumped into an electric cattle fence. I about jumped to all four feet yelling, "You rotten little chunk of mutton!"

I could see him in the moonlight as he backed away, turned, and ran down the deer trail toward the pasture. I bolted down the trail after him yelling, "Get back here!"

Mepos kept on the deer trail all the way to the pasture fence, making no real effort to lose me in the moonlight and deep shadows. It was almost like he wanted me to keep sight of him as he ran. His behavior made me suspicious.

Still, he did not pause to open the new gate. Instead, he climbed between the fence wires and once through, ran as fast as he could through the pasture up to the gate by the barn. I increased my speed to a full gallop, wishing I had thought to grab my iPhone so I could have called Aunt Bonnie for an intercept.

Up by the barn, he slowed at the gate, climbed through between the rails. "Come on, slow poke."

That challenge made it obvious he did not want me to lose track of him. I jumped the new gate and charged across the pasture, totally taking him by surprise enough to force him to bolt past the barn and up the short drive to Aunt Bonnie's house.

Closing on him quickly, I spotted him running through the side and back yard. He made a sharp left and headed toward a weathered old garden shed half hidden behind vines and locust saplings on the edge of a stand of woods just beyond the freshly mowed lawn.

The building was Aunt Bonnie's original garden shed, but she had abandoned it five years ago when she put in a bigger one that held the John Deere Gator and her garden tools. The old shed was not in very good shape and had a sagging, rust-streaked metal roof.

Mepos disappeared in the moon shadows near the dilapidated building and I swore I saw him slide sideways through the woodshed door. I rushed up to the shed, skidding to a stop, listened a moment at the door, then yanked it open, wishing I had a flashlight. I quickly discovered I really did not need one.

Right across from the open door against the back wall was a large floor to ceiling storage cabinet nearly as wide as the whole wall with double doors. Bright light showed all around the door seams. I stared at it, and then cautiously stepped into the shed, hearing the wood floor squeak and groan in protest under my weight. Feeling like my hooves would break through at any moment; I took three steps which took me all the way to the cabinet.

Cautiously, I opened both doors to find a thick curtain of leafy vines blocking daylight. The desperate need to check things out fought with caution. I tentatively reached out to the vines and pushed them aside just enough to see what was beyond them. It was a whole different world of open forest and glen full of wildflowers bathed in daylight.

"Oh, hell no!" I breathed, backed up, let the vines fall back in place, and closed the cabinet.

I hurried out of the shed and went directly to Aunt Bonnie's back porch. I clumped up the stairs and rang the doorbell.

The second she opened the door, I blurted out, "I found the portal!"

Her eyes went wide and she clutched lightly at her chest in total surprise. "Where?"

"In the big storage cabinet in your old garden shed, there." I pointed into the darkness. "Followed that little mutton head, Mepos. He woke me just a little while ago. When I chased him, he ran just slow enough to make sure I was following him."

"I haven't been in it for years. It was going to have it torn down this summer. Don't, under any circumstances, go through that portal until we find out more. I'm locking all my windows and doors. You did not mention . . . you know . . . to him?"

"No way," I said.

"Good. I don't think we are in any real danger, yet. But no matter what happens, we have to be extremely cautious."

"Do you think it is safe for me to sleep in the hut?"

"I think you'll be fine. He does not seem to be hostile. But who knows what else is in that reality? I'm getting Frank's shotgun out of the gun safe and keeping it handy, just in case."

"Okay."

"I'll see you in the morning at the barn. Sleep well." She closed the door.

I headed back to the hut, my thoughts drifting to what Mepos said about not keeping the bow strung. I wondered what made him such an expert on archery. It bothered me. I did not sleep well.

Fitful sleep was haunted by nightmares of knocking down jumps, shooting arrows at black helicopters, being chased by some gigantic thing I could not identify. Just crazy stuff I don't really fully remember, except for the last dream.

In that one I was held fast by the portal tangle of vines in the storage cabinet. The more I struggled, the tighter they gripped like leafy pythons. I was trapped between two worlds and was yelling for Aunt Bonnie. I only woke up when I became aware of something poking me rather hard in my horse ribs.

When I opened my sleep filled blurry eyes, I just made out something large standing in the hut entrance in the gray light of dawn. I rubbed my eyes with my fists and refocused.

There in the entrance stood another centaur. His human part was built like a lightweight WWE wrestler and dressed in a leather vest with matching leather bracers on his wrists. His face was handsome and aquiline with a short beard, but his hair was rather long, like a rock star, and he was frowning at me. The horse part was light but strongly built, and I could not tell the color except it was dark. In his right hand was my bow and he was ready to poke me again with it.

"Get on your feet, Jerry Swift," he commanded in a resonant voice. "I am Chiron. You are in obvious need of learning the proper use of this fine weapon, a gift from

Artemis. And remember, when the student is ready, the teacher will appear."

I scrambled to my feet, staring at him in total awe. "How? Why? I'm not a Greek hero."

"Follow me and bring your quiver of arrows. Less talk and more attention to what you are doing." He turned away.

My immediate impression was that he was a strict teacher and would not answer any of the million questions that instantly popped into my head. Including the mind-blowing fact, the bow was from Artemis, a daughter of Zeus and goddess of the hunt.

I followed him a few yards until he stopped. He snatched the quiver from me and thrust the bow into my hand in a swift, rough manner. Then he hung the quiver from a branch within reach.

He looked at me standing there watching him, shook his head, and grabbed my left hand, put it on the bow grip and roughly manipulated my fingers to a proper grasp, took my right hand and pulled it to the bow string. "Grip the string and pull it back to about your ear."

I did the best I could, my muscles burning to the point my arm shook. I just barely pulled back to the position he wanted before I gave up and let the string pull my hand back to the starting point. I looked at him and smiled weakly, totally embarrassed.

He looked at me and shook his head again. The sun was just reaching the eastern horizon, and he continued to stare at me, disappointment showing in his dark eyes.

In that second, he took the bow from me, grabbed an arrow from the quiver, nocked it, and let it fly at the target in the woods across from us. I was amazed he made a perfect bullseye in the low light.

"You will be able to do that once we strengthen your arms. For now, you will lift weights with both arms every day. Put rocks in a sack and lift it with each hand in turn twenty times every morning and night for a week's time, adding two fist-sized rocks every day until they reach the weight of a child of three years and we will try again." He unstrung the bow. "Put this away until then and retrieve that arrow."

"Can I ask why I have to learn this? I'm trying to find a way to . . ." I started.

"We know what you are trying to do. And we know of your sister. You are helping her is admirable. But this is all more complicated than you know right now. There is a strong possibility you will need to protect yourself and those you love. And you may also need to hunt for food. That is all you need to know for now. Work hard."

"What about Mepos?"

"Artemis and I sent him to deliver the bow and quiver of arrows and so you would know of the portal. Tell him nothing. He means well, but talks too much. I will, however, tell you now that he is partly responsible for the loss of the . . . object. I must go now." He put his right hand on my human shoulder, squeezed it, turned, and galloped away, becoming a dark bay colored equine shadow that lost itself in the long darker shadows of dawn and left me with more questions than answers.

Now I had two assignments: get ready for a jumping certification test and bulk up my pitiful arms to handle a bow from a goddess that could save us from some unknown danger.

11
Tests

For the next week, between my academic studies getting ready for finals, lifting the sack of rocks, and practicing over the jumps in preparation for the certification test, I was exhausted by the time night came. However, I was very thankful Mepos kept away. . . or at least I thought he did. I really would not put it past him to spy on me and did not need him complicating my life.

Oh, I did not tell Aunt Bonnie, or my friends, about Chiron at our Wednesday game. I did not want even more questions that could lead to more complications or temptation to explore the other dimension, family and best friends or not. It would be too dangerous for them and probably really piss off Chiron.

However, the first thing at our game Aunt Bonnie did after putting up her Dungeon Master's screen was to say, "We do have a bit of news we should tell Ben and Alice."

"What news?" I gulped, my stomach feeling like it dropped twenty stories as I took my gaming notes out of a folder that I kept in the barn office. I could only think she either saw Chiron or Mepos came back and paid her a visit.

Ben and Alice looked on anxiously.

"The noise outside the window last week was a faun by the name of Mepos spying on us. You should keep an eye out for him when you are here. I suspect he is trouble," Aunt Bonnie finished. "I'm keeping my house locked up at all times, and just had an alarm system put in."

"Holy crap!" Ben blurted out.

"Is he looking for the stone?" Alice half whispered.

"We don't know," Aunt Bonnie returned in a low voice. "Don't talk about it. Especially if there is any possibility of him being around listening. And don't mention him to Ann or anyone else."

"He told me he was here to help set things right when he showed up at my hut and gave me a bow and quiver of arrows," I went on.

"Very curious," Alice commented.

"For hunting or . . ." Ben added.

I felt I had to change the subject and stupidly blurted out, "Can I tell them about the portal?"

"You just did." Aunt Bonnie laughed. "Turns out there's a portal in my old garden shed between our world and his. I would not consider exploring it if I were any of you. It might endanger getting Jerry back to his old self. There is so much we need to find out before we consider a scouting expedition. Agreed?"

I could not help frowning as my earlier thoughts came back to haunt me. Though they meant well, the last thing I wanted was everyone tramping into an unknown world right out of the pages of Homer's *Odyssey*. Especially if the Ancient Greek monsters were real and by all indications, they probably were. At least Aunt Bonnie seemed on the same page as me.

My friends both looked annoyed and grumbled unconvincingly, "Okay."

Alice frowned deeper and burst out, "No! I take it back. We have to do something. We have to check it out. Maybe if we find Mepos over there, he can help us get to the bottom of all this and we can get Jerry back to his old self."

I knew Alice was a fighter, but I had to kill the idea and mood it fostered fast and was angrier than ever at myself for mentioning the portal.

"Listen. It's for our own good, guys. We don't know what's out in that dimension and you can bet there are monsters only unlike our games, there is no saving throw. And I'm not all that good with a bow and arrows. In fact, I suck."

Ben perked up and cried, "Hey, man. Maybe we can catch Mepos here, get him drunk on wine, and question him. They do like to party hardy according to the myths."

Alice laughed.

"I already suggested that," I said.

"I don't think it is a good idea. It could open a bigger can of worms than we are already trying to deal with," Aunt Bonnie broke in. "Let's pick up where we left off last week in the game and get our minds off our real world for a little while. Maybe it will inspire our search for answers to our real-world issue."

We had a good game that night, killed a small war party of Orcs, found treasure, and took a break to discuss rolling up another character each to make our party of adventurers stronger rather than rely on the non-Player Characters. Aunt Bonnie believed it could be a good idea and wanted to think about it. Our night ended without any *Twilight Zone* interruption.

The rest of the week went by quicker than I wanted. I was distracted by two worries: Chiron showing up again Friday in the wee hours or late in the evening to give me more archery lessons and, most of all, the jumping certification test Saturday.

Especially when I saw that Aunt Bonnie and Mrs. Albert added three more jumps, a triple spread, Swedish oxer, and a four-foot high and ten-foot-wide faux grass jump. The test was set for ten Saturday morning. I was really happy I got to sleep all night and woke up around six with no Mepos or Chiron showing up.

I had a pancake breakfast with Ann and Aunt Bonnie in the barn at seven. Ann was wearing a white polo shirt, tan riding breeches, tall black boots, and had her riding helmet handy. Time seemed to slow down to a crawl like it always did before a major test at school.

At 9:30 a.m., Mrs. Albert arrived and talked to Aunt Bonnie outside by the arena while Ann gave me a quick brushing and got all the tack on me, including helping me with the deer stand safety harness with the reins over my freshly washed lucky black *Star Wars* T-shirt. Neither of us spoke.

Then, out of the clear blue, when she finished adjusting the saddle girth, Ann said, "Stop worrying about our practice course being changed. I know that's what's got you so quiet. I get to walk like before this test and every show course like all riders do so I can physically count strides between jumps to be able to make a plan on how to ride the course. For your genius brain to calculate, a horse stride is twelve feet."

"Thanks for that bit of info for my math calculations." I smiled, though it did little to soothe the anxiety.

When we left the barn to meet Aunt Bonnie and Mrs. Albert by the jumping arena gate, Mom and Dad drove up, to my total surprise. I had figured they both might be working.

They got out of the car and when Dad saw my confused look said, "You didn't think we'd miss this, did you?"

They hugged us both. Then we waited by the arena gate while Ann walked with Mrs. Albert around the course. I noticed Mrs. Albert had a clipboard in hand. Though I watched them, my mind kept drifting with my eyes towards the edge of the forest for any sign of Chiron or Mepos.

I knew I had to forget everything that went on outside the arena and put my full attention on the jumps once the test started. It would only take us two minutes at most to get through the course, but it would be the toughest two minutes of my life. I did not want to fail my sister. I looked away from the woods and concentrated on Ann.

It was hard to guess what she was thinking as she walked past the last three jumps with a perfect poker face. There were eleven jumps in all and in different locations from yesterday, except for the Liverpool jump.

When the walk through was finished, I heard Mrs. Albert say as Ann buckled on her helmet, "Ann, I want you and Jerry to make two exercise circuits around the neighboring arena to warm up and then enter here at the gate and start your run."

Ann just nodded, came directly over to us and stated bluntly, "I hate this course."

"Why?" Aunt Bonnie asked.

"Why?" I echoed as she mounted.

"It starts up as a figure eight, then shifts in a hard left to an extra loop," she explained.

"Hey, a turn is a turn," I said, trying to blow off the worry. "Are we timed?"

"No, but as you know we have to do this without knocking anything down and keep at a steady pace through the whole course," Ann grumbled.

"Nothing different from what you have in the show ring, Honey," Mom said.

"No pressure . . . not. But at least it is not like that Grand Prix nightmare on YouTube you insisted I watch." I took a deep breath and turned when Ann instinctively tapped her boots against my horse ribs out of habit and lightly tugged the reins of my safety harness as a signal to head for the other arena to warm up.

I could not help thinking if Chiron was watching from the woods, he'd probably be having a fit if centaurs were like those in the *Harry Potter* books that refused to have a human on their backs. We were both silent during the exercise.

I forced my thoughts to concentrate solely on the next few minutes in the jumping arena. I thought the best idea was to just let her take over, making all decisions on getting through the course.

"Ann, just signal me like you would Gold Coast. I'll not argue or try to do anything on my own, okay?" I asked.

"I hear you, but I will talk to you. I always talked to Gold Coast, though I know he did not understand my words. It just made me feel better and maybe calmed him when needed. He could get a bit wound up at times," she replied.

We stopped as we reached the open arena jump gate and looked over at our family. Mom came over and patted my horse shoulder. "Remember, deep inside, we all can fly."

Ann touched my human shoulder. "Ready?"

"Ready as I'll ever be," I returned.

"Let's start at a slow canter for the first simple jump and keep that pace. Let 'er rip!" she shouted.

I took off and broke into a slow canter and sailed over the rail fence, clearing it easily. I had the feeling the ease of it was a way to induce us into being complacent about the rest.

"Wall," Ann announced, though I saw it plainly looming ahead as she touched my horse ribs with her heel to signal more speed on the last few strides.

I put on a little more speed and effort into the jump since it was built of light blocks that would fall at the slightest touch. I made it over with inches to spare.

"Triple combination with two strides between them. Be careful," she said as I saw we were approaching three rail jumps that looked to me like they were set too close together on the first curve of the s-shaped section of the course.

I got over them, but I brushed the top rail of the last jump with the bell boot on my left front hoof. I heard the rail wobble precariously behind me, but it did not fall.

After a sharp turn right, I got over a descending oxer followed by an ascending oxer. Then we headed left for a hogsback jump, and I got over that without an issue. I felt Ann nudge my ribs with her heel for more speed as she warned. "Triple spread coming at us."

Before I knew it, I was upon three rail fences set close together to force a long jump. I pushed off the ground hard, tucking my front legs right against my horse chest. I barely missed touching the top bars.

After two strides, Ann signaled to turn sharply left to a simple rail jump. Then we were headed to the

Liverpool. That took another hard leap and stretch. I just missed the edge of the pool in my landing.

We were then headed for the x-shaped Swedish oxer, which despite the optical illusion of being tall, was not a major problem as I sailed over the middle lower point at the center of the X and on to the last jump in the test: a faux grass jump. I went over that one, jumping high enough not to get tickled.

I can't tell you the intensity of the relief I felt making it through that obstacle course. As we stopped after the last fence, Ann leaned forward and grabbed me around the back and chest in a hug, yelling, "We did it! Oh, thank you! Thank you! Thank you!"

Our family was waving at us from the gate as Mrs. Albert wrote on her clipboard. I trotted over with Ann still on my back, clinging to me.

Mrs. Albert looked up at us with a grin. "Very good. A couple of close brushes, but I'd say you finished the test with flying colors. I just have to finish the paperwork and you'll have your certification. Congratulations, you two."

With everyone so happy about the certification results, I hated to be a wet blanket, but I had a question pop up in my mind that had to be asked. As soon as Ann slid off the saddle and hugged our parents and Aunt Bonnie, I walked over to Mrs. Albert. "What if the USEF refuses to okay this because I'm not a real horse? Hasn't anyone thought of that possibility?"

"Jerry, I have," Mrs. Albert said. "Otherwise, I would never have agreed to go through with all this. I am looking at it in the light that you are all horse where it counts, and this is certainly tougher and more dangerous than a school track and field competition. All health papers are about ready, all equipment is regulation and you and Ann have passed your competency requirement.

"Besides, I know most of the important people in the USEF. We are all avid horse enthusiasts. As a backup, I took the liberty of filming your competency test with your parents' permission. I will not let anyone copy it or let my iPhone out of my hands when I show the needed evidence to the USEF, and show chairman, and anyone else who needs convincing."

I looked around at everyone. "What if someone kicks up a fuss? This is not going to remain a secret for very long. I don't want to get stuck in a media circus the second I set a hoof on the Kentucky Horse Park grounds like I mentioned before."

"Don't worry, Jerry. We'll handle it," Dad broke in. "There may be some media picking this up, but it will work to our advantage. Too many people will be around for anyone or organization to bother you at the show. Any criminal activity like kidnapping takes time to plan. It is only a two-day show and not a big Grand Prix event with Olympic champions competing that draws a huge crowd.

"The Park is expecting three thousand spectators at most. You will be accompanying Mrs. Albert with Drama

Queen in her big van with dressing room and you will be in it and not a barn open to the public. Besides, from the ground, many people looking at you two from the rear will think you're just another horse and rider. For extra security, I'm renting a camper to park on the property campground, and your mom will be with me. We will stick close to you during the show."

I thought for a second. "You could be right. Odds are it should work." I knew well the operative word was "should."

"Well, to celebrate everyone is invited to our cookout at six tonight," Dad announced.

"I've got to get back to writing and Jerry, in about ten minutes, Peg Anderson and Gladis Phibs are due here to pick up their horses for a show. So. you'll have to head out to your hut."

"I'll cool myself down on the walk to the hut, so don't worry," I mentioned when I saw the concerned look Mrs. Albert gave me.

"I'll see you tonight at the cookout. Again, good job you two," Mrs. Albert said and left.

"Hey, can I come with you to your hut?" Ann asked as she took the saddle, breast strap, my helmet, and deer stand harness to the tack room.

"I don't see why not." The words were out before I could stop them. I hoped Mepos or Chiron would not show up with her there.

The two of us walked down to the woods in silence. I got the creepy feeling we were being watched, but said nothing to Ann. I only hoped whoever it was that they would stay out of sight.

"This is not too bad," Ann said upon walking into my hut for a look around. "Where'd you get the cool bow?"

I was forced to lie. "I made it from stuff I found in the woods and what Aunt Bonnie gave me. Have to do something besides home schooling on the computer in the barn to keep from going nuts. If I'm still stuck in this body by deer season, I plan to do a little hunting. Centaurs need meat and a lot of it, along with other food. It will lower my grocery bill to hunt."

"That makes sense." She poked me in the horse ribs playfully. "Explains why you eat like a horse now."

"Ha! Ha! Very funny. So, I don't eat hay and oats," I came back.

"Well, it's not your room out here, but at least it looks comfortable. I better get back to the barn and get Gold Coast out on his walk. See you tonight. And thanks so much for doing this with all the risks."

"You're my sister. Family is supposed to help family. Right?"

She hugged me and headed down the deer trail.

The cookout went fine. Dad had gone all out with Angus sirloin steaks purchased from one of our neighbors. Mrs. Albert brought a huge bowl of mixed greens salad with tomatoes and Mom made a ton of potato salad. Everyone was in a party mood over our getting our Show Jumping Certificate of Capability.

Our get together did not break up until ten. By then, I was stuffed and sleepy. The last thing that Aunt Bonnei informed me was that I'd have to spend the night out in my hut since one of the boarders was coming to pick up their horse for a trail ride with friends first thing in the morning. I did not mind, figuring on a visit from Mepos or Chiron by then.

All the way back to my hut, I had the feeling of being watched again from the darkness. When I reached it, I went in and just stood waiting and listening rather than snuggling down with my quilt in the bedding. I heard dried winter leaves crackling and the thud of a four-footed walk. I peeked out. In the pale light of a half waning moon, I saw Chiron's shadowy form.

"Good evening, Chiron," I called out.

"It is about time you got back," he said gruffly. "We have work to do. It is too dark now here. Bring your bow and quiver and follow me through the portal."

I gathered up my things and did not dare complain of being tired from the jumping test, all the worry over exams, and the threat of discovery hanging over us all. Besides, my curiosity over his world was about to be solved and I would not have to risk snooping alone. Not that I would, mind you. But I intended to tell Aunt Bonnie, Alice, and Ben what it was like to cool their curiosity and keep them from doing something stupid.

I followed him through the woods, skirting the pasture over to Aunt Bonnie's yard and continued to the old garden shed. He went in first and I followed, noting the big cabinet double doors had been left open to the curtain of vines.

The moment I went through the vines, I was hit with bright daylight and forced to squint for a moment. We were in a small open grove of young oaks spread wide apart where only moss and some weeds grew below their broad canopies.

Now that we were in daylight, I noticed he had a bow and quiver over his shoulder and over the other what looked like a leather messenger bag. Before I could ask a question, Chiron was next to me and grabbed my right arm, pinching at the muscles, checking them and not too gently, by the way. He did the same to my left.

"Some improvement in tone. String your bow," he ordered curtly.

I handed him the quiver of arrows. He took it and watched me with sharp eyes as I placed the strung end on the ground and bent the other end to slip on the string into the notch, dreading I would not have the strength. To my great surprise, I accomplished the task easily, noting my arm and back muscles did not twitch or burn at all.

"Very good." He smiled for the first time. He took a pair of bracers from the bag over his shoulder. "Put these on to protect your forearms."

I handed him the bow and pulled on the bracers, finding they fit perfectly.

He handed back the bow, took an arrow from my quiver, and handed it to me, then pointed. "See that massive oak tree over there with the blackened knot in the middle of its trunk?"

I spotted it. It had to be eighty yards away. "Yes."

"That is your target. Shoot."

As much as I wanted to make a comment, I did not dare. I nocked the arrow and took nowhere near the effort I used when I first attempted to pull back the bowstring. I aimed, taking into consideration the slightest breeze.

I let the arrow fly. It hit the top edge of the knot, but it was in the black. I looked over at Chiron. He had the hint of a frown on his face and looked at me.

"Well, at least you hit the tree." He handed me another arrow. "Again."

I sighed and took it. On my second attempt, I hit the knot almost in the middle.

"Much better," he said, but he was not yet smiling. He handed me the quiver. "Put this over your shoulder and go retrieve your arrows."

I nodded and left him. On the walk over, I could not help looking around at my surroundings. One sun was in the sky, and the area looked no different than a state or national park wilderness in my world.

We were in an open field of tall grass and mixed wildflowers with a couple of oak groves. There were many young trees with a few giants among them like you would find in an old growth forest; great massive trunks and thick leafy branches reaching for the sky.

The portal was a shallow cave in a hill with a pile of huge boulders marking the entrance on which grew vines with a few scraggly pine trees pushing out of cracks. Far in the distance there was a range of snow-topped mountains that would challenge the Rocky Mountains of the Southwest.

They made me wonder if the real Mount Olympus was up in them. When I reached the tree, I pulled the arrows out of the knot and turned to walk back to Chiron.

Two things happened simultaneously that nearly blew my mind. I saw him suddenly grab his bow, nock an arrow, and was aware of a shadow approaching from above and to my right, accompanied by a God-awful scream and the smell of rotting flesh. Breath caught in my throat. I turned in time to see an arrow hit what could only have been a Harpy in the chest and it crumpled in midair falling to the ground.

Two more of the ugly half women, half vulture creatures followed in an attack; one at Chiron and the other straight at me. Their image would forever be seared into my brain of a naked woman's upper torso and twisted human face, with a predator's teeth and hair replaced by long feathers blending into a huge black vulture body having wings instead of arms and vulture feet with talons that could do serious damage.

I immediately nocked another arrow and let it fly. It went through the creature's wing, spinning it in a cartwheel to the ground. Chiron's arrow hit the one diving for him through its skull, dropping it like a stone.

In a flash, he put another arrow into the chest of the one I had hit when it struggled to its feet and came at me again, running and flapping its good wing. It dropped dead barely a foot from me, its red eyes staring right through me as life left it.

In shock, I looked at Chiron as he trotted over to me.

"This is part of what I warned you about and the reason you must become a competent archer," he said, taking another look at the sky before focusing his attention fully on me. "Hermes probably sent them."

"Can I ask what exactly is going on?" I said nervously, my heart still racing from the attack.

"A stone that belongs to Circe has been stolen by Kyriako, the brother of Mepos, on the order of Hermes. It is the stone she uses in her spell to turn men into beasts. He lost it in your dimension when he accidentally fell through the portal while trying to hide in what he thought was a cave and did a little wandering.

"We knew the stone was near you when you became a victim. This was seen in a scrying session by one of our seers. It is lucky your enemy chose the words he did. Had you been called a horse, that is what you would be and not have drawn our attention by being one of us. We would not have known where to start looking."

"Isn't it considered to be an insult to be called a horse's . . ." I started, but he waved off the question.

"Not really. However, we centaurs are interfering to keep Hermes from starting a war with Circe. We are healers and seers. Hermes is an arrogant fool out for power and a known thief and meddler. The bad blood between Hermes and Circe goes way back.

"Hermes helped Odysseus win over Circe by giving him the moly flower that would prevent her magic from taking effect on him. Thus, Odysseus seduced her and got his crew changed back to human. Why Hermes wants the Changing Stone is anyone's guess. Mepos got involved because his brother has been captured by Circe, who has threatened to kill him if the stone is not returned by the next full moon. The gods are playing this as a nasty game, as usual, which indicates they are probably bored. At least Artemis and Pan are on our side and helping where they can."

I just stood there, open mouthed and awestruck by the story. It made perfect sense. "My aunt Bonnie and I have been trying to solve this mystery for the last couple of weeks. We were right about a few things. But most of all, I need to be changed back to my old self. Well, maybe after I help my sister in that horse show." Despite my misgivings, I said, "I've got to tell you something in full confidence. Is it safe here to talk?"

"There are other ways of communicating among us who are trained in the metaphysical arts, and Hermes is not skilled in it." He placed his right hand gently on my head. "Think what you wish to tell."

My thoughts rang out. *We found the stone. My aunt Bonnie has it hidden in her attic.*

He nodded. Then his thoughts came back clear, as if he were speaking to me. *Tell her to give it to you. I will come for you tomorrow evening and we will get it back to Circe. It will not be an easy task, but we have little time, and I think you are up to it.*

I nodded, I understood and he took his hand away.

"Now it is time to get you back to your world," he said and turned away.

I followed, knowing this was all going to open a new can of worms I really did not need with exams coming up and, in a few weeks, the full moon in his dimension and the horse show. But if there was any chance I could have the curse broken, it would be worth it.

12
Almost Kidnapped

Sunday I woke up just as tired as I was when I went to sleep. I could not get what Chiron had told me, or the living images of the Harpies out of my thoughts. It all hit home harder than ever that there were other dimensions now that I had the time to internalize everything since that adrenaline rush from the battle had left my system. It rattled me to the core of my being and proved we lived in a Multiverse instead of a Universe.

However, I knew all too well that any physicist, including my father, who dared write a paper on a dimension where Greek myths and magic exist, would be considered ready for the rubber room despite Einstein's famous quote, *"The mind that opens to a new idea never returns to its original size."*

I went down to the barn rather late and on the way saw Aunt Bonnie and Ann in the first light of dawn release the three boarding horses still at the barn into the pasture since it was a nice warm day. I jumped the back-pasture gate and trotted toward them, waving. They waved back.

As I reached them at the barn gate, Aunt Bonnie held it open for me. "Was beginning to wonder if you got lost."

"No, just overslept," I said, aching to tell her what happened, but knowing I could not at the moment in front of Ann.

"Sleeping is his favorite hobby," Ann cracked.

"I wish," I shot back.

"Are you two up for some home-made waffles from my grandma's old waffle iron?" Aunt Bonnie smiled knowingly.

"You bet," I returned, feeling my stomach growl at the prospect.

"Hope you have enough batter. You'll need it with him joining in," Ann came back, not missing a beat, and gave me a playful smack on my horse butt when I passed her coming through the gate.

"Just remember who's helping you toward the Olympics," I fired back.

"Oh, that burned," Aunt Bonnie commented, and we all laughed.

I followed them up to the house and waited at the back porch. While they were busy getting breakfast, I could not help looking off toward the old, dilapidated garden shed. Having that portal so close had me worried more than ever after last night.

Oh, the whole structure looked innocent enough in the tall grass and the spring wildflowers that buzzed with bumble bee activity showing no hint of what was inside.

But anything could get through and the Greek myths had plenty of other monsters to worry about besides the Harpies.

On top of that was a psychotic god who might choose to make an appearance. I felt guilty for not telling Aunt Bonnie about Chiron and our experience with the Harpies last night. But what could she do?

Board up the doors or burn the shed down? One wrong guess, one wrong action, and this whole mess could blow up into a worse clash of realities. My imagination went wild at that point; part of the problem of having genius intelligence.

My worries all boiled down to a simple truth. All the military might in our world meant nothing when faced with true magic that seemed to be the way of natural law in that other reality, and the fact it was spilling over into our dimension.

It was a sobering thought. And worst of all, it started giving me the feeling a confrontational crisis was looming. We were stuck in the middle of what amounted to a tiff between a messenger god with a bad case of hubris and very powerful sorceress and the gods and goddesses that sided with her like in a *Dungeons and Dragons* adventure.

But.

This.

Was.

Real!

Aunt Bonnie's voice from in the kitchen brought me out of my thoughts. "Ann, go down to the barn office and get me another dozen eggs out of the egg fridge, will you please?"

"Sure," came Ann's answer. She bounded out the kitchen door to the porch and looked over at me in passing. "Can I hitch a ride? It'll be quicker."

"Your legs work fine," I shot back in mock sarcasm. "I'm not your equine taxi service."

I swear I saw her stick out her tongue at me on the shadowy porch as she turned to run for the barn in the weak dawn light, giggling all the way.

That was only moments before I heard Mepos yelling from the woods near the barn, "Run! Run!"

Then there came a blood curdling scream from the other side of the tree lined driveway near the barn that about stopped my heart.

Ann!

With a deep sense of mortal danger, I bolted across the backyard and down the driveway. The shrieking continued another second before it was muffled. As I approached the barn at a full gallop, I peripherally spotted a large bipedal and horned shape with Ann under its right arm headed for the woods in the dawn shadows.

A freaking Minotaur!

"He's taking her to Hermes who wants you out of this!" Mepos yelled from behind a tree. "I tried to stop him . . . with my slingshot."

I heard Aunt Bonnie come out on the porch, turned to her and yelled, "Get the shotgun!"

It was the closest weapon that would do any real damage. I had done skeet shooting before, long story for another time. I knew how to handle a shotgun a bit better than my bow.

Then I galloped back to the porch. There was only one place the Minotaur could head, and I intended to block the way. It took a moment for Aunt Bonnie to show with the shotgun, and I snatched it from her with the words, "Sorry, no time to explain."

I galloped from her toward the shed, intent on blocking the creature's path into the portal as soon as it came out of the woods, noting the shed doors had been left wide open. I could hear weighty footfalls approaching in the surrounding woods along with heavy breathing and the muffled screams of my sister.

A huge horned biped shape emerged from the woods only twenty yards from the shed. At ten feet tall, the Minotaur was every bit the nightmare man-bull of the legend, heavily muscled, naked except for the slick short black fur over its shoulders, neck, bull head, and bovine tail.

It had Ann under its right arm with a huge left hand over her mouth and face. It regarded me with baleful yellow eyes and roared a warning, lashing its bull tail.

Mepos was suddenly behind him and let fly a near fist-sized stone from his slingshot that hit the Minotaur in the back of his head. The huge beast just shook his head as if it was a mere fly bite.

I took a step toward him, raised the shotgun and yelled, "Drop her or I'll blow your freaking head off!"

I knew it probably did not understand my words, but it must have understood my intent from the tone and raised shotgun. Ignoring another slingshot attack by Mepos, the Minotaur broke off a thick sapling and strode forward, ready to use it as a club on me. I took aim at its head, forcing myself to hold fire until the very last moment to lessen the chance of Ann or Mepos being hit, and pulled the trigger a second before I was within reach of the tree trunk club.

The Minotaur bellowed in pain as it swung the club, forcing me to scramble out of the way while I pumped in another shell. Mepos ran for the woods. I glimpsed the damage. The shot had turned part of the right side of the Minotaur's face to hamburger, including the eye that was now a bloody hole. But that did not stop it and it did not drop Ann who had fainted and hung limp under his arm.

The Minotaur staggered for the shed with me at too awkward an angle to attempt another safe shot at its head. As it went for the storage closet, breaking through the floor at one point, I managed to get directly behind it and fired at the left side of its back at close range away from Ann. Gore flew everywhere, and the beast staggered and fell through the vines into the other dimension.

Deep, bellowing groans sounded from the other side of the portal. I did not hesitate for one moment. I dropped the shotgun and bolted into the shed. With only the section of broken floor slowing me, I dashed through the vines. I almost fell on the prone, unmoving bloody monster's body, dodging at the last second. Ann was on the ground a few yards from him, having rolled a little from where he had dropped her when he fell.

I instantly went to her, knelt, and scooped her up in my arms.

Mepos burst through the vines, a look of shock on his face, and almost tripped over the huge body. His eyes wild, he bleated in fear. "What sort of magic was that thunder that killed a Minotaur?"

"A shotgun. Got no time to explain more," I said, turning for the portal holding Ann tight to my chest, my left hand supporting her head and I whispered to her, "Ann, I'm so sorry. You're going to be all right. I promise."

The Minotaur suddenly reanimated and grabbed at my left hind leg with its right hand while trying to push itself up with the left, but collapsed dead with a rattling, gurgling sigh the second I reached the vines. Mepos squealed and followed me.

I pushed through the vines, stopping only to close the big cabinet doors with my right hind leg after Mepos came through and half stumble through the shed on the broken floor. After he passed me, I closed the shed doors behind us again with my right hind leg. Not that it would do any good. Aunt Bonnie was waiting on the porch, her face pale and hands gripping the rail so hard her knuckles were white.

"Oh, my God, bring her here, quick!" she called frantically. "Is she alright?"

I clambered up on the porch, and we sat her in a lounge chair as I said, "She might be a little bruised, but should be okay, however mentally she will probably be in shock."

"I saw most of what was going on. What is he doing here with a Minotaur?" Aunt Bonnie glared at Mepos.

Mepos spoke. "I tried to stop him with my slingshot. Hermes sent him to kidnap Ann as a threat to make all of you stay out of things. Chiron sent me to warn you, figuring Hermes would not be suspicious about a missing faun on our side since we often drink too much wine and sleep it off hidden away."

Aunt Bonnie's eyes went wide, and she said sternly, "First you and now this. And Chiron? Jerry, you have some explaining to do while I get her some water."

She rushed into the kitchen, letting the screen door slam behind her. I looked at Mepos.

"She doesn't know about Chiron, does she?" Mepos asked sheepishly and backed up one step.

"No, I chose not to tell her, but now I have to explain everything. This is all getting way out of control," I shot back savagely. I was frustrated. I thought I had a handle on this whole mess and was angry at being proven wrong. Control over anything was always an illusion.

Ann started to stir as Aunt Bonnie returned with a glass of ice water.

"You better go back and go fetch Chiron. I'll meet you by the portal on your side." I shot a sharp look at Mepos.

The faun nodded and ran for the shed just as Ann sat bolt upright in the lounge chair.

"Take some water, Honey. You're safe now," Aunt Bonnie said, passing her the glass.

"What the hell is going on?" she cried, grabbing the glass, her hand shaking and a few stray tears sliding down her cheeks.

"Jerry, is Chiron who I think he is?" Aunt Bonnie demanded, glaring at me. "Let's have the whole story right now."

Well, I spent the next ten minutes explaining everything that had happened over the last few days. I ended with, "And don't worry about Mepos. He's on our side. And speaking about our side, I need to get that stone back to Circe. That is the key to the whole mess. Maybe she will return Mepos's idiot brother, Kyriako, and perhaps change me back if Chiron talks to her. This must be done before the full moon over there, or Circe will kill Kyriako and who knows what Hermes will try next. And I have no idea of what the moon phase it is on their side of the portal."

While she sipped the water, Ann stared at me as if I had gone around the bend yet hugged herself protectively with her free arm. When I finished, she blurted, "I don't ever want to see one of those Minotaur things again! God, I feel so violated. That Mepos is not much better."

Aunt Bonnie took the empty glass and hugged her, kissing the top of her head.

My strategy suddenly shifted course slightly.

"Aunt Bonnie, you may not approve of this, but I need that stone like now. I'm going back through the portal and return it to Circe. Got to end this *now*. I'll give you the shotgun and go get my bow and arrows first. It might be a good idea for you and Ann to go to our house until this is over. You can explain it all to Mom and Dad when they get home if I'm not back by the time they arrive from work," I said, fixing them both in a steady gaze.

"You know I don't like this one bit. It's not one of our *D & D* adventures. There is no saving throw." Aunt Bonnie stared at me; her mouth fixed in a grim straight line. She went into the house without saying another word.

"I'll have plenty of help," I replied loud enough for her to hear.

Ann's eyes were filled with fear. "Don't do anything stupid. I need you. We need you. And thanks. And thank the weird goat guy, Mepos, when you see him again."

She got up and ran down the two stairs to hug me around my waist with her cheek against my belly. I put my arms around her, feeling her tears soak my t-shirt. Then she let go and backed away as Aunt Bonnie came out to the porch with the messenger bag, in which she normally kept her laptop, and the tin with the stone. She put the tin into the bag and came down the stairs to put the bag strap over my shoulder.

"Since you don't have pockets, this will have to do." She smiled tremulously and hugged me. "Please be careful."

I nodded, trotted over to where I had dropped the shotgun and brought it back to her. "Go to our house as soon as you can and promise to keep this with you at all times. Don't let our parents call the police or anything like that. They can't do anything that could make things worse. And don't tell them about the portal being in the shed."

"I promise," Aunt Bonnie answered stoically.

"The police wouldn't believe us anyway, and would probably have us tested for drug use," Ann cracked, brushing away tears.

Aunt Bonnie put her free arm around Ann's waist and guided her to the porch stairs. She looked solemnly at me. "Jerry, you stick close to Chiron and do what he tells you."

"I will," I said, turned and galloped for my hut to get my bow and quiver of arrows.

13
Dungeons and Dragons for Real

I skidded to a stop at my hut, picked up the bow, and slung the quiver over my shoulder. My mind and emotions were spinning out of control. One thought that came through was if anyone told me a year ago that this is the life in store for me, I'd have told them to seek psychiatric help. The urgency of my mission squelched it almost the second it hit. Then I galloped along the wood lot edge to the shed, extremely alert for any other ambush Hermes may have arranged.

I found Mepos had left the shed and the cabinet doors wide open. I stepped through the vine covered portal to find the sun going down on the other side and both Chiron and Mepos waiting by the bloodied body of the Minotaur torn even more by scavengers as ravens and vultures circled overhead.

"What manner of weapon did you use on the beast?" Chiron demanded.

"A shotgun. It is a projectile weapon that uses explosive powder to shoot multiple projectiles into a target. Very effective. There are many similar weapons in my dimension," I responded.

"I can see that it is effective," he said. "You did not bring it with you?"

"No. I left it with my aunt Bonnie so she can protect herself and Ann against anything else Hermes sends to my dimension."

"Wise move." Chiron started walking with Mepos through the meadow toward the thicker woods away from the bloody carcass. "We have a way to go to get deeper into these woods to find Pan who can get us to Circe's Island, Aiaia. This is a bit awkward for him to go against his father. But then again, rebellion against wayward parents is not all that unusual around here with gods, mortals, or other beings in disagreements."

"If I remember the story as it came down in my dimension, Hermes impregnated a Dryad and she gave birth to Pan," I said, following him.

A brief smile ran away on Chiron's face. "The acorn does not fall far from the oak. Hermes was the result of Zeus not being able to keep it in his tunic around the beautiful Pleiad Maia, eldest of the seven sea nymphs that are companions of Artemis."

"I'll have to thank her for the bow. This whole thing is getting more convoluted by the moment. I sure hope Zeus does not get involved," I added, feeling a cold seed of fear in my gut.

"He has a hands-off attitude, allowing others to handle his brat unless it gets really serious, which I'm afraid may just happen from all the warnings of our seers," Chiron went on. "Stay alert to our surroundings."

"Sounds like what's going on in my world with most of the football team bullying my friends and me because we are gifted intellectually. Their parents do nothing to stop it. That's how I got changed thanks to Andrew Collins taking that stone from me," I groused, noting the forest's old growth trees becoming more numerous and closing in on us, making it dark as twilight with their far-reaching canopies.

It was not long before the woods took on the look of an old growth northern rainforest like those in Washington state and Oregon with lush ferns, vines, and mosses growing thick everywhere that were not covered by massive trees. Trees that would take several men with spread arms to reach completely around the trunks' diameters. Again, my vision was almost as good as if I was wearing night vision goggles, which was probably a centaur thing, so I did not have to worry about tripping over a log or an ambush by some monster.

I knew horse vision was excellent in the dark. I figured that the attribute was even more pronounced in this dimension. I heard the calls of insects in the underbrush as thousands of lightning bugs flashed semaphore signals all around us. Far in the distance an owl called.

I became so hyper alert that the least motion had me staring at any shadowy ferns or vines that moved. The deepening shadows seemed full of unseen creatures, more so than any summer camp night hike.

It was hard to figure distance, but after an hour by my watch I figured we must have gone at least a couple of miles, and the forest started to open a bit to an area where massive boulders the size of a cabin laid scattered in an overgrown glade. Mepos, who was walking a few yards ahead of us, suddenly stopped to sniff the air.

"I smell something and it stinks of carrion," he half whispered, and reached for his slingshot.

Chiron instantly nocked an arrow in his bow and I followed suit, suddenly smelling the same rotten meat stench with bad body odor, like opening a locker to find dirty clothes left for a whole weekend. My heart began to pound and breath came short. My every nerve was on edge.

Ahead on the other side of the closest boulder, something weighty crushed branches under heavy foot falls. All I could think of was there was another Minotaur or two.

"Spread out," Chiron ordered.

We did so and none too soon. To a deep growling grunt, a stone the size of Aunt Bonnie's John Deere Gator came flying over the massive boulder to crash on the very ground where we had been standing grouped together. It was followed by a high wild laughter and the words, "Drive the meddlers before you. Kill them if you must."

"Hermes, you are mad as a spring hare!" Chiron yelled at the voice.

I glimpsed something man-sized flitting through the air to disappear in the dark forest canopy. Then, a split second later, a Cyclops strode from behind the massive boulder, shoving oak saplings aside as if they were shafts of wheat with hands the size of the average dining room table.

The height of a four-story building, the primordial member of the race of giants had skin that looked more like stone. A twisted, ugly scared face on a head topped with matted hair on a short thick neck and a chunky torso with bare barrel chest supported on pillar-like legs ending in bare feet with toenails that were more like claws that finished off the immediate impression.

His only clothing was a loincloth of dirty cow hides. He focused his one bloodshot eye on us and bellowed loud enough for me to feel the force of it all the way to my spine.

Mepos bleated in panic and disappeared into the darkening underbrush.

"Oh, shit!" I yelled, ready to run and join him.

"Aim for his face and let fly!" Chiron commanded. "I prefer not to kill him and risk the wrath of Poseidon, who has fathered many of them with sea nymphs. It should discourage him from following us."

"And if not?" I drew back on my bowstring.

"We circle in opposite directions and keep firing at his head and neck until he runs," Chiron said, drawing back and letting his arrow fly.

I let my arrow fly, too. Chiron's hit him square on the tip of his crooked bulbous nose and mine hit him on the cheek, to the left of his eye. He staggered back, bellowing in pain, his eye watering profusely.

Chiron trotted one way and I the other around the Cyclops, firing several more times. Our six arrows hit him in the face and neck. Bellowing even louder, the Cyclops tried to slap the arrows away as if they were angry hornets and pulled several out, blood streaming down his face.

It was like toothpicks being fired into a pumpkin. All we were doing was pissing him off. He bellowed and uprooted an oak tree. He swung it at us. We were both forced to retreat about fifty yards.

The Cyclops kept coming and threw the tree at us, forcing us to retreat further. The tree was deflected by a massive moss-covered oak, the impact sounding like a clap of thunder followed by the wooden smacking of falling branches.

At that moment, the the sweetest flute music that I ever heard floated in to rise above the sounds of breaking brush and snapping limbs as its melody grew ever louder in the twilight. I was overcome with an intense lethargy that sapped the strength from all my limbs.

In moments, I sank to the forest floor. My last thought being I was going to be crushed by a tree or under a monster's foot any second, but strangely I was at such peace that I did not care as I fell into a deep sleep.

14
The Magic Stone and Promises

I was awakened by someone shaking me by my human shoulders. My mind screamed out Cyclops, registering that I was about to be eaten alive or torn to pieces and I swung hard with my right fist. My wrist was grabbed as I opened my eyes to focus on an older, robust adult version of Mepos with smiling dark eyes, short dark beard, curved goat horns that looked like they could do serious damage and along with it all the earthy scent of goat mixed with human sweat.

"Pan?" I mumbled loudly.

"Easy, young one. You are all right," Pan spoke. "I had to put you all to sleep with a tune from my pipes for your own safety."

It was then that I noticed behind him the Cyclops was flat on his back, snoring and drooling.

"He will be out a long time. We must leave and put as much distance between him and us as possible," Pan said as I got to my feet. "Follow me. I have a way to get you to Aiaia and have arranged for you to meet Circe. Well, she knows you are coming."

I quickly noticed both Chiron and Mepos were on their feet, alert and ready to go.

"Let's hope your father does not send any more creatures to stop us. That is getting a bit old," I complained.

"You did quite well for yourself." Chiron nodded at me. "Don't sell yourself short, Jerry Swift."

I noticed a sly smile on Pan's face. "I don't think Hermes will cause us much trouble."

"Oh?" I trotted over to him, ready for his explanation as we followed him down a deer trail in the thick old growth forest.

"Artemis is seeing to it that he keeps away from us for quite a while," Pan returned.

Mepos uttered a giggle that sounded more like a goat's bleat. Chiron smiled knowingly.

"Am I missing something?" I asked, not happy to be out of the loop.

"Artemis, daughter of Zeus, goddess of virgins, the hunt and wild animals, and protector of women, and young creatures, has taken a liking to you for the sacrifice you are making for your sister. She wants to help us all in our quest to end this trouble Hermes, her thieving half-brother, has started before it devolves into more violence between the Olympians. She has introduced him to some very nice nymphs that are keeping him quite distracted in a chase, and I believe one or two dryads are also involved. If you get my drift." Pan gave me a lecherous smile and winked.

"I get it," I said and felt my cheeks go hot.

Mepos giggled even louder.

We followed Pan silently through the deep forest until the gibbous moon rose when we came upon a dreamy glade that looked like something out of a Renaissance painter's creation. Moonlight fell in shafts through the forest canopy to sparkle on the wings of flying night insects, and the surface of a small pond fed by a spring that bubbled out of a hole in the center of a large, flat boulder on one side.

"This is a portal to the island of Aiaia for those who know how to use it. It opens in an identical pond on the other side. The portal entrance is between those two clumps of cattails across the way. You only have to simply walk into the water until you are almost covered, take a deep breath, and hold it as you continue under the surface, and you will instantly come out in a pond on the other side," Pan instructed.

It reminded me of the flue system in the world of *Harry Potter*. "It's that easy?"

"Of course. Not everything in this world is a major challenge. Though I must say whatever does not kill you here makes you stronger."

"Now you are starting to sound like Chiron," I cracked, and got smiles from both in return.

We followed Pan to the cattails on the other side of the pond. I must admit I was feeling just as nervous as if I were called down to Principal Archer's office.

Pan looked over his shoulder at us and went on, "I'll be coming with you at the request of Artemis."

That made me feel a bit better, knowing Circe's reputation from the myths we read in literature class. He walked into the pond first, and then Mepos followed by Chiron, all continuing in until their heads disappeared below the surface. When it was my turn, I stood for about three heart beats staring into the clear water. The bottom appeared solid.

Reluctantly, I took two steps into the pond, feeling the sandy bottom firm under my hooves. I took a few more steps until the cool water reached my horse belly.

The bottom was still firm under my feet. The only thing that made me move quicker was the heavy tread of feet crackling through the brush deep in the woods on the other side of the pond.

The Cyclops. That was the only thing it could be.

I walked quickly further into the pond until only my head was above the water. I took a deep breath, and another step as my head dipped under the surface. I was instantly hit with the sensation of falling, as if I stepped off the edge of a cliff.

My dark, watery world spun me over and off my feet, making me lose some air in bubbles. Just as suddenly, there was solid sandy ground under me. I instantly found myself stumbling and staggering out of the pond and gulping air that had a sea tang to it in a twilight forest on the Island of Aiaia. Pan, Mepos, and

Chiron were waiting on the bank for me, still dripping water from the experience.

"It's about time. We thought you got lost," Chiron cracked, and swished his tail splattering me in droplets.

"The Cyclops is coming through the woods," I warned, and shook water from myself.

"Well, we need not worry here. He won't be able to follow us. Cyclops hate baths," Pan assured us with a wry smile. "Come with me."

We followed him along a narrow trail deeper into woods much like the one we had left. The trees soon opened onto a large clearing in which stood a beautiful mansion of white stone with Doric columns that put me in mind of some of the buildings I saw on a school trip to Washington, DC. The path to the mansion was lit by fires in bronze bowls atop white marble pillars.

Around the house prowled strangely docile lions and wolves who I knew to be the drugged victims of her sorcery. They were not dangerous, and fawned on us, asking to be petted.

As I walked, I looked around for Kyriako, but he was nowhere to be seen. The woman I figured to be Circe was up on the portico attended to by an attractive nymph while she worked at a huge loom in the light of many hanging oil lamps and a large glowing globe the size of a basketball that hovered near her.

She was as stunning as her legends described. Raven ringlets cascaded down her shoulders from under a golden tiara. When she looked at us, her dark eyes missed nothing in a face of classic Grecian beauty.

She was dressed in an Ancient Greek style chiton; a large rectangular piece of fine linen dyed a pale blue bordered with a geometric design in gold embroidery draped over her body to cover the left arm, but leave the right free. The back and front were fastened at her shoulders with gold broaches, the front draped low and was quite revealing. A gold and jeweled girdle gathered the chiton at her slim waist.

She motioned with her right hand for us to come closer and in a lilting, strong voice said, "I have been expecting you and your friends, Lord Pan."

We drew closer, yet stopped at a respectable distance at the bottom of the four marble stairs. Some of the wolves and lions drew closer. Mepos half hid from Circe between Chiron, Pan, and me in a most guilty manner, looking nervously at the predators that were slowly surrounding us.

"The moon grows fat. Have you found and are returning what has wrongfully been taken?" Circe continued.

"Jerry," Pan whispered, motioning for me to step forward.

Mepos dove under Chiron to stand on his other side.

"I have it here, my Lady Circe," I said politely, digging into my messenger bag for Aunt Bonnie's tin box, my mouth suddenly dry.

I took out the box and carefully climbed the stairs to the porch, holding it out in my right hand, noticing a particularly large lion approaching to my right in my peripheral vision. As I reached her, I bowed slightly, keeping eye contact, not really knowing how to properly greet her.

She looked at me with gentle eyes and took the tin box from my hand. When she opened it, her smile lit up her face and made my heart skip a beat, I swear.

"This is truly the lost gem." She gently lifted it out of the box and placed the container by the side of her chair as she stood.

I suddenly saw the eerie foxfire blue green at her touch. She looked at it in a fulfilled manner, then at me. "You have been an unintended victim, Jerry Swift of Greenville, Kentucky. I know your wish to return to your original human form. Yet, there is conflict in you. The promise you made to your sister. It is something beyond the love we call phila: a love between siblings. Yours goes deeper to a love we call agape which embraces a universal, unconditional love that transcends and persists regardless of circumstances. It goes beyond just emotions to the extent of seeking the best for others; absolute love."

It was as if she could see all that had happened, but then she was a sorceress, after all. Still, it made me extremely uncomfortable. I could only nod my head to acknowledge the conflict churning in my heart. I could see no way out of it.

"I have a way of solving this," she said and closed her right hand over the gem, holding it out to me along with her left hand balled in a fist. She stopped and closed her eyes, mumbling a spell in what I took to be an Ancient Greek dialect.

When she opened both her hands, the gem was in her right hand as perfect as ever, but had become a pendant on a gold chain. She quickly slipped it over her head to rest on her bare chest. When she opened her left hand, in it was a ring with a smaller yet perfect copy of the original moonstone.

"For your bravery, sacrifice, and honesty, I give you the reward of this changeling ring. It is only for your use and will allow you to change at will between the centaur you are now and that of your original human form with only a voice or thought command as long as you wear it. Use it wisely." She closed the distance between us and slipped the ring on my left middle finger.

The second it touched my skin; I felt a static shock like you get in the winter when you touch a doorknob after walking across carpet. I smiled as I took a closer look at it, finding it made of silver with tiny Greek writing around it I could not read.

"Thank you."

I caught her smile. "Well, Jerry Swift, try it out."

"Um-m-m, I don't have any pants . . . err . . . clothing to cover up . . . you know." I was suddenly embarrassed.

My companions laughed out loud, as if I had just told the greatest joke in the world.

"You have nothing I have not seen before. But for the sake of your modesty." Circe snapped her finger at her nymph attendant. The nymph bowed, quickly walked away, and came back with a fine white linen chiton and handed it to Circe, bowing again. Circe spread it over the rear half of my horse body. "Now, make your wish."

I handed Chiron my bow, quiver, and messenger bag, then made the wish, got terribly dizzy and fell almost blacking out completely. When my full senses returned, I found myself sitting on the marble porch wrapped in a pile of linen from the waist down in my old body with everyone staring at me.

"How do you feel, Jerry Swift?" Circe asked, leaning over me with her hand on my shoulder.

I looked up at her, wiggled my toes and answered, "Dizzy, but great. Thank you."

Mepos and Pan clapped and Chiron beamed while all around us the wolves howled and lions roared. Circe stood up to her full height, raising her hands, and the howls and roars died away.

"Now, about the thief, Kyriako," Circe said darkly.

I saw Mepos cringing next to Chiron. In a low, strained voice, he pleaded, "I tried to stop him . . . I tried to talk to him out of it . . . please don't kill him."

A stony look came over the sorceress. With a wave of her hands, Kyriako appeared out of nowhere on his goat knees and in chains on the marble porch a few yards from me. His eyes were red and face drawn. He looked like a slightly older version of Mepos, but there was something sinister about him.

"Kyriako . . ." Mepos said. "Kyriako, why?"

"Does it matter?" Kyriako spat out the words, his face twisted in anger to an ugly half-human mask as he stared at Mepos with a searing hate in his dark eyes and his goat ears pressed back at an angry angle, making him appear demonic.

"It does to me," Mepos came back on the verge of tears. "You are my brother."

"Do you think I want to spend my life like you, a simple forest creature when a god promises so much more?" Kyriako raged.

Circe glared at him. "Then you will spend the rest of your life in service to a god. I'm sure Dionysus could use a strong worker in his vineyards. As a little extra punishment, you will find all wine tastes like vinegar if you decide to take a free sample and nymphs will forever shun your advances. That will be your curse," she proclaimed, waved her hands, and Kyriako vanished.

She turned a kinder face to me. "It is time to return you to your world. Chiron, Pan, and Mepos will escort you through our world in your centaur form. Remember, the ring is for your use only. No one but you will be able to make it work. I wish you and your sister luck in the long quest for the Olympics in your world. It is a most noble pursuit.

"And I will see to it no one else but Mepos, Chiron, your patron gods, or you can get through the portal in the structure that belongs to your aunt. Goodbye, Jerry Swift of Greenville, Kentucky." Before I knew what was happening, she stepped closer, reached over to pull my face closer to her, and lightly kissed me on my right and left cheeks.

I felt my ears go hot and knew my face was probably deep red. Everyone, including Circe, laughed at me. Still, it was a big relief to hear the portal would be protected, putting to rest the very same worry that sprang instantly into my mind.

As instructed, I tried the ring again, and the change was instantaneous with the annoying dizziness and pain of muscles and bones growing that were not normally there. I staggered to my feet, a bit disoriented, but the feeling passed quickly.

Chiron handed me back my bow, quiver, and messenger bag. Circe let me keep the chiton, which I folded and put in my bag. It did not take us long to walk to the pond as night closed around us.

"It might be wise to let me go first just in case the Cyclops is still there," Pan said.

"I agree," Chiron added.

Pan jammed a stick in the ground in a moonlit spot and put a pebble a little distance from the moon shadow it cast.

"Give me that much time, and then follow," he instructed and walked into the pond.

I sighed. Mixed emotions coursed through me like a stream ready to overflow its banks as I watched Pan's horned head disappear below the water's surface. My thoughts jumped to thinking about going home and taking up my life again, and what it would be like being able to shape shift into a centaur at will. It was crazy and risky as hell, but I had a promise to keep to Ann no matter what it put into motion in my world.

15

Family Reunion, Exams, and Jock Trouble

Soon it was time to follow. I went last and the second I broke the surface; I heard loud snoring. Just beyond the reeds by a huge boulder, the Cyclops lay on his back, snoring and drooling. Fur and hair still damp from the trip, Pan, Chiron, and Mepos stood by the reeds waiting for me.

"So, he was waiting," I commented as I walked toward them, dripping wet.

"Yes. His kind are as fond of fauns as they are of human flesh and since he probably smelled the scent of faun by the water, it made sense he would be waiting. They are very persistent hunters, and my father depended on that fact. We had better be on our way." Pan headed for the deer trail we had used to reach the pond.

I cast nervous glances at the sleeping monster as we trotted past. We kept up a swift pace with no one talking. Overhead, the tree canopy blocked out most of the moonlight, keeping the forest in deep darkness, which made it hard to guess the time. Curious, I checked my watch to find it four in the afternoon in my world.

When we reached an area where the trees were not as massive, Pan stopped and turned to us. "This is where I leave you. Good luck, Jerry Swift. We may meet again." He shook my hand, then turned to Chiron. "Just follow the deer trail. You will soon recognize the territory."

"Take care, old friend," Chiron said and they shook hands.

Pan jogged away to disappear into the dark forest.

I continued on with Chiron and Mepos to the rocks where the portal was hidden. I could smell the location long before it was even in view. The jumble of boulders was silvered by the gibbous moon.

Below it, I could see the huge carcass of the Minotaur with dark shadows moving around it. Some I recognized as wolves as we drew closer. Others I was not so sure what they were. Everything scattered at our approach and fled into the night to become shadows within shadows.

Just to be safe, Chiron and I each nocked an arrow and Mepos put a stone in his slingshot, ready for any trouble as we walked closer. They stayed with me right up to the vine covered entrance.

There I returned my arrow to the quiver. Chiron only loosened the tension on his bow string long enough to be able to hold the bow and nocked arrow in one hand and shake my hand with his free one. "The best to you, Jerry Swift. Be careful in your world."

Mepos shook my hand. "Good luck, Jerry Swift."

"We will see you again," Chiron said.

"I'll miss you guys," I remarked.

He nodded, and backed away, taking up his bow to stand guard with Mepos at his side.

Feeling a catch in my throat, I ducked through the vines and was quite surprised to see a new plank floor in the shed in the late afternoon light pouring through the open shed doors. I stepped onto them quite sure it was Circe's magical work by the hand wrought iron nails I spotted in the boards.

I turned around and closed the cabinet doors behind me to find a very strange Ancient Greek tumbler lock manifest itself on the hasp. I left the shed, closing that door behind me, but nothing happened on its hasp.

Heart racing, I immediately headed through the woods toward the back porch of my house with no idea if anyone was at home. I saw my parents' cars parked in the drive and my heart leaped.

On the edge of the woods, I took off the quiver, bow, and messenger bag, pulling the chiton out. I stared at the ring, made my reversal wish, and fell to my knees dizzy.

I did not black out when I shrank into my human body, but it was not a pleasant sensation. Shrinking meant horrible cramping and it almost made me wish I had blacked out. Maybe this was how shape shifting in my world was going to be so I would not use the power in a frivolous manner.

I sat there naked in the grass, a bit stunned, and then pulled the chiton around me. Holding the chiton in place, I slowly stood erect and for a second, the world stopped spinning. I picked up my bow and quiver, slinging them over my shoulder, and put the messenger bag over my other shoulder and walked barefoot to the porch.

I quietly padded up the three stairs and rang the backdoor bell. The door slowly opened. I stood silent in the wash of the late afternoon sun, looking like I had arrived home from the Peloponnesian War wrapped in the chiton. First, I saw the barrel of a shotgun and then my father's face that instantly broke into a broad grin.

"Jerry! You're alive!" he yelled. "And you're back to yourself!"

Before I could say a word, Dad, Mom, Ann, and Aunt Bonnie burst out of the kitchen and hugged me in a massive group, all talking at once. I was swept away in a storm of mixed emotions; joy, love, relief, but it was tinged with sadness. The sadness became apparent the second I was released and saw the look in Ann's eyes as she fell silent before the rest of my family.

The excited questions stopped. I reached out, took her hand, and looked into her teary eyes. "This does not in any way mean I will not fulfill my promise. We have worked too hard to quit now."

"But how can you?" she asked.

"Let me tell you all the whole story from the time I went back into the shed," I said and we all retreated to the kitchen where I spent the next half hour in a blow-by-blow report that sounded more like something Homer might have written.

When I finished, Ann asked stoically, "Well, when are you going to use that ring to turn back into a centaur?"

"Right after exams. They start tomorrow and last for two days. I'd really like to go to school to take them and let everyone know I'm okay. The process of shape shifting, like I said, can be painful. Then I plan on staying in the centaur form until after your horse show so I can continue jumping practice and be ready to compete. Or at least that seems the most logical course right now," I answered.

Ann immediately hugged me. I did not miss the questioning looks from both parents and Aunt Bonnie.

"You better put that ring in a safe place. We do not need a repeat of the stone incident," Mom suggested.

I nodded and tried to take it off, but it would not budge. I knit my brows and looked at my family, feeling as if my stomach dropped to my feet. "I believe it is magically fused to me. Circe has made sure no one else can use it. I should have figured she'd do something like that, given her reputation."

"Then I'd think seriously about taking your exams online. You don't need to run into a problem at school with that Collins kid trying to take that ring. You know it will tempt him," Dad warned.

"After all I have been through fighting monsters, I think I can handle a human bully," I said, quite confident at the moment. "Chiron was an awesome teacher. He had me doing things I thought I could never do in a million years. Maybe you will meet him someday."

Everyone let the subject drop. The rest of Sunday got back to near normal. After a welcome hot shower, I spent most of the rest of the afternoon on Facebook messaging with Alice and Ben, which was great.

That evening, the whole family went off to a celebration dinner at the Blue Door Smokehouse in Lexington, one of our favorite restaurants. Later it was great sleeping in a real bed, though it was in our guest room off the family room downstairs. Mine had not yet been replaced.

I got immediately back into my school morning schedule and for probably the first time in my life, I was happy to go down our drive to wait for the bus with Ann who was all secret smiles, probably thinking of the horse show. I had an excuse note in my pocket from Mom with a forged doctor's note on stationery I made up on my computer that looked identical to that found in any doctor's office.

Its creation was about as close as I ever want to get to being an evil genius. As soon as the bus stopped at school, I was off to the office to get an excuse slip that would let me back into my homeroom class.

On my way, every teacher I knew greeted me, saying they were glad to have me back and wished me well on exams. Looks I got from students I knew were mixed. My best friends treated me like a rock star in the hall when I passed them at their lockers. Others were lukewarm, and the jocks were totally surprised. A few glared mysteriously angry and I mean the kind of glares that would translate into "I-wish-you'd-drop-dead."

When I asked Ben and Alice what was going on by their lockers, Alice explained. "You know how we hate passing on gossip. We did not tell you at the last game that Gina Howard's detective dad let it slip to her that you disappeared because you were kidnapped by unknowns as a hazing move, dumped in Daniel Boone National Forest, and were too traumatized by the experience to come to school or talk to anyone, except your therapist. She told her friends and you know how it goes. Half the school thinks it was someone on the football team, and the rumors are chipping away at their overblown pride and pissing off Thornton and Archer."

"This could get ugly," Ben added. "We better stay close to you both to and from our exams since we'll all be in the same room and especially at lunch."

"Sounds like a good idea. Strength in numbers," I said, thinking Mom and Dad were right. I should have taken the exams at home.

We went to exams right after homeroom. Our first exam of the day was College Calculus and Trigonometry with College Physics due to be given after lunch. The exam was not bad. Lunch quickly became a whole other story.

Just when I thought all would go well with the jocks off in a whole different hall in the school for exams with the general population of students, Andrew and three others on the football team were in the lunch line just ahead of us when we entered the cafeteria. I looked around the room and spotted our police officer and a few teachers on lunchroom duty, which gave me the needed confidence.

When Ben and Alice balked at the cafeteria entrance, I kept heading to the lunch line. "Come on, they don't own the cafeteria."

Alice caught up quickly and grabbed my arm. "It might be better to wait until they are through the line."

Ben walked up. "I think she's right. They've been getting in our faces on and off since you've been gone and Archer ignores our complaints."

I smiled ever so slightly. Actually, I think it was almost a smirk.

"Listen, I have faced Harpies, a Minotaur, and a Cyclops. I refuse to be intimidated by a jock anymore. We have backup. Let them get stupid first and maybe someone will finally do something about them."

Grudgingly giving in, Alice and Ben followed me to the line with me letting one girl in ahead of us as a buffer and Alice got ahead of me. We stood quietly, trying to blend in as a few students came in behind us.

The jocks were all busy talking about the math exam and putting food on their trays when Ed Foster pointed us out to Andrew with a nod of his head.

Andrew looked over his shoulder right at us as he stopped by the fruit counter and narrowed his eyes.

Then, in a voice loud enough to be heard by those in the immediate area, he snarked, "So the Geek Squad is back together again. What's the ring for, Swift? You get engaged to Brunhilda, your beefy Valkyrie protector while you were recovering from your little trauma?"

I saw Alice's face go red and before she could make a comment, I said in a loud enough voice to be heard in the immediate area, "Alice, don't let the brain-dead Neanderthal annoy you. He only knows how to trash talk, and we should pity him for his great lack of critical thinking."

She paused by the pizza with me right behind her. She glanced at me over her shoulder and smiled. She then spoke in an equally loud voice, "You're right. He should be pitied for his lack of critical thinking."

I saw Andrew's hands clenching his tray so hard his knuckles went white and his face flush. We had dared to stand our ground and that would not be allowed with all the witnesses around. I could smell his adrenalin rise; a left-over attribute of being a centaur, I instantly reasoned and was ready for his reaction. It was speedy in coming.

He grabbed an apple and threw it brutally hard at my head. I could have blocked it with my tray as a shield, but after training with Chiron and fighting monsters, my reaction was totally different. I grabbed the apple right out of the air like cat quick as it passed Alice's head, and I threw it back hard. It exploded on Andrew's forehead and knocked him off his feet with food flying off his tray everywhere before anyone knew what was happening.

A shriek sounded from in front of him, followed by a giggle that could not be stifled, and I noticed it was Andrea Baker. She went to him and helped him sit up, but she could not stop giggling as she took a chunk of apple out of his hair.

One of the teachers on lunch duty, Mrs. Rose from the English Department, came over and admonished, "That was very ignorant and immature, Mr. Collins. And Mr. Swift, you were not much better. Consider this a warning. Anything more and you will be doing lunch detention tomorrow. Now get your lunch and move on to separate locations to eat. We will be watching."

Mrs. Rose got on her radio, glaring at us. As the jocks moved on with Andrea and Andrew arguing, we gave them a few minutes to get well ahead, allowing other students to pass us.

Ben put his hand on my shoulder, beaming like a Cheshire cat. "I don't care what she said. Man, that was awesome, and he deserved it. Just love it when Karma hits immediately."

"Well, as awesome as Ben thought it was, I don't like the way Andrea keeps glancing over at you," Alice grumbled.

I looked and unfortunately caught her eye. She had that hungry look when a girl was thinking of going astray from her boyfriend. I quickly focused on Alice as she helped herself to some pizza. "I just saw what you saw. Could mean trouble I really don't need."

She looked up at me and smiled. "Well, your arms and chest have sort of bulked up a bit and you don't look so wimpy since the change, probably thanks to Chiron."

"Thanks . . . I think," came my lame answer.

We had a peaceful lunch and afternoon exams went well. But when I went to check my locker for books that still needed to be returned to my classes, I found a note taped to the door. It had Andrea's name and phone number in purple ink with flamboyant handwriting.

I stuffed it in my jeans pocket really quick, looking around hoping Andrew had not seen it. In no way did I plan on calling her. I wanted nothing to do with that kind of teen drama and needed to stay in one piece for the horse show. Assuming we would be allowed in.

16
The Inquisition

After school, while Ann took Gold Coast for his exercise walk, I took my bow, quiver of arrows, and messenger bag down to my hut. I must say, the trip seemed rather strange on two feet instead of four and took longer. I went to the barn to make sure my iPhone was in the charger in the office and checked my laptop.

While I was in the office, I heard Aunt Bonnie come into the barn with Mrs. Albert and left the office to see what was going on. They both looked over at me as I closed the door.

"Good, you're here," Aunt Bonnie said.

Mrs. Albert looked at me oddly. "Sorry, it's a bit strange seeing you back to your normal self," she said awkwardly and smiled.

"We were just talking about the last weeks up to the show," Aunt Bonnie continued.

"A glitch seems to have developed," Mrs. Albert added, her eyes suddenly avoiding mine.

"Glitch?" I questioned; glad Ann was still outside with Gold Coast.

"Mr. Craig Braddock, President of the USEF, and Mrs. Anita Stone, the show chairlady at the Kentucky

Horse Park, and some of their board members want to see you and Ann before they agree to allow you in the horse show. Regardless of the video, your health and certification papers being in order, and all equipment being regulation." Mrs. Albert sighed. "I'm sorry. I thought I could have them convinced this was all real and legal. Apparently, I was wrong."

My heart felt like it dropped to my feet with that news. Now this was all becoming an inquisition and to me, about as bad as the historic one. Yet I suppose I should have expected it.

"When do they plan on showing up?"

"Tomorrow after school at 4:30 P.M..," Mrs. Albert returned. "They wanted to settle this as soon as possible. It's all for the best, I guess."

"Did you tell Ann yet?" I asked.

"We were on our way," Aunt Bonnie replied.

I sighed deeply. It all meant that as soon as I got home, I'd have to go to the barn and shape shift when I wanted to not have to do it until the following day so I could have one more full day in my original body with my family. "She should be fine with it. Me, not so much. It's making me feel like a freak."

"Well, think of it this way," Aunt Bonnie said. "They will not be in total shock when you show up at the event when they are expecting a horse. It may lessen the possibility of a total media circus and possible panic, plus they will have warned security, so you get some protection."

"Maybe," I said half-heartedly. "But promise me you will let me explain how I got this way by a cursed stone, and say nothing more about the whole true story. Play dumb."

"They already know about the stone," Mrs. Albert put in. "I think they just don't believe it happened that way. Most adults have a hard time wrapping their minds around magic that is real and not stage magic or something out of movies or books. It blows their minds to think it could be real.

"I sometimes think they believe I'm perpetrating a hoax with computer graphics. My own sanity is being questioned at this point and reputation, though I offered to take a drug test. I have just as much to lose as you do. Show jumping is just as large a part of my life as it is for Ann. More so, in fact."

I fully understood and nodded. They left the barn to talk to Ann.

Dinner was quiet. Ann and I just picked at our food. I got little sleep with my mind running through various scenarios of the meeting. I always had the habit of over thinking things, like I mentioned before.

My last three exams in English Literature, World History, and College Astronomy and lunch mercifully went by without incident at school the next day. However, last thing of the day during dismissal, Andrea waved at me in the hall as I headed with Ann to catch our bus.

I did not return it. In fact, I did my best to ignore her. I would not be coming back for the last three days of school and was supposedly returning to therapy for PTSD from the hazing, so that would end her quest.

Still, Ann saw the wave and had to ask, "What was all that about?"

"Never mind. I will not be seeing her or the Neanderthals at all the rest of this week or next year, as they will all be gone to college. End of story," I shot back as we boarded the bus.

"I think she has the hots for you since you bulked up a bit and made her 'bae' look like an idiot yesterday," Ann came back, a devilish twinkle in her eyes that told me she was having fun pushing my buttons.

"It's not mutual, so drop the teenage drama. We have enough on our plate this afternoon with all those officials showing up like this was the freaking Inquisition and we are the witches." I settled into watching the new spring green world pass by out the bus window as it pulled away from the high school.

As soon as we arrived home, we went our separate ways; Ann to get dressed in her riding attire and me to the barn to go through the change. Aunt Bonnie was up at her house fussing in her garden and waved at me.

I waved back and headed for the barn office to undress. I left all my clothes neatly folded on the desk and walked out to the box stalls, naked except for my lucky black *Star Wars* T-shirt. All the horses were out in the pasture except Gold Coast, and he nickered at me as he put his head over his stall door. I patted his neck as I passed him, heading to the stall I used and closed the door behind me.

"Well, here goes," I muttered, looked into the moonstone on the ring, and wished to be a centaur again.

The pain was not as bad this time, but I still dropped unconscious into the bedding. When I came to, I had all my horse parts back again. When the dizziness left, I was able to get up on my feet. I shook myself like a dog and swished my tail. I checked my watch.

It was 3:50 P.M. I stepped over to my stall door to wait for Ann to come get Gold Coast for his exercise walk since we had time. She came in the barn, gave him an apple, and clipped on his halter rope.

"Want to come with us?" she invited.

"No, I think I'd better wait here out of sight. You can bring that committee in the barn when they arrive." I folded my arms, leaning on my stall door. They were important yet unwanted guests, as far as I was concerned, hoping this was all not going to turn into some freak show with the media possibly being called in.

I watched her lead Gold Coast out of the barn and go around the corner. I knew her routine. She'd walk him around the barn four or five times, and then take him to a lush patch of grass over by the pasture fence. She came back in at 4:15 P.M. and I heard Aunt Bonnie and Mrs. Albert talking to several people coming down the drive from the house. Ann quickly put Gold Coast in his stall and stepped over to mine.

Aunt Bonnie came into the barn with Mrs. Albert and six other people and stopped just inside the barn door. There were two men and four women. One slim middle-aged man dressed in casual riding attire had to be the president of the USEF, Craig Braddock.

I'd seen a picture of him before in one of Ann's show catalogs. I was not sure of the other heavier man in a casual suit and hair in a buzz cut. The women ranged in age from thirty on the low end to fifty or so on the high end and all were dressed in casual office clothes, except for the oldest one I guessed to be the park show chairwoman Anita Stone, also in casual riding attire. All of them were staring at Ann and me.

Mrs. Albert announced, "I assure you, ladies and gentlemen, this is no hoax. Jerry, come on out."

I just nodded. Ann stepped out of the way. I pushed open the stall door and strode out into the broad aisle under the harsh glow of florescent lights to the sharp intake of breaths. They stared at me wide-eyed. Mr. Braddock's jaw dropped.

"Close your mouth, Craig, before you catch flies," Mrs. Albert cracked, and broke the tension.

"Inconceivable," Mr. Braddock finally said in a low voice, and took a tentative step toward me. "May I . . ."

"I know, check me out," I finished with a slight sarcastic edge to my voice. "Feeling's believing and I'll just have to get used to it."

He cautiously lifted my t-shirt to check where both bodies joined, ran a gentle hand down my left horse shoulder, and along my back as everyone watched his every move and mine. I swished my tail for good measure. He went around, checking my hooves and legs as I expected him to do.

He stood back and looked me over. "You know that little video was phenomenal, but not even close to meeting you. Still, I'd like to see you two run that course in the arena, if you don't mind. And I am sure that's true with the rest of us."

"No problem," I came back.

"Sure." Ann smiled nervously.

"Oh, Jerry, that is Mr. Braddock, the USEF president. This is Mrs. Stone the park show chairlady in charge of all horse shows, this is Miss Gilbert her office manager, this is Mr. Stewart head of park security, Mrs. Dobbs assistant to the head of park security, and Mrs. Ryder the park CEO," Mrs. Albert made introductions. I could hear the relief in her voice and hoped it was not premature, given we just shoved a lot of people right into the *Twilight Zone.*

Aunt Bonnie and Ann got me all saddled, helped me get the deer stand harness on, and I did not forget my helmet.

"That is one strange rig," Mrs. Stone commented, pointing to the deer stand safety harness with the reins attached as I adjusted a strap.

"Substitute for a bridle. The reins still allow steering signals and allow me to do something with my hands to keep good form," Ann explained.

"I just let her do the commands and try not to interfere," I added. "This is all a lot harder than track and field, and I was never the athletic type. But that's kind of changed with the curse."

"That curse story is kind of farfetched," Mrs. Ryder stated coldly.

"Sure, until you find yourself a victim of one," I replied, a bit waspish, not liking her attitude. "All I want out of life is to be a Cosmologist. Study dark matter, string theory, and quantum mechanics versus general relativity; maybe discover something new about the creation and existence of the Universe and Multiverses.

"I'm used to dealing with exotic theories where there is no evidence they exist in physics. Magic may just be a branch of physics, along with the existence of other dimensions. The Universe is stranger than anyone who is outside the world of physicists can believe. I have just discovered there is more strangeness in the Universe than even physicists like my father know. I recognize full well what has happened to me pushes the envelope of what we know about nature. But more important, I have a promise to keep if I'm allowed to do so."

Mrs. Stone and Mrs. Ryder gave us dark looks.

"Go warm up," Mrs. Albert butted in before things could take a bad turn.

Ann and I went out to the jumping arena to do a couple of slow canters around the jumps for warm up exercise. The rest followed us, talking and debating the issue in a garble of voices that put me in mind of a seabird rookery.

I did manage to hear Mrs. Stone's complaint, "His human intelligence will put the other horses at a disadvantage."

When we reached the group on our last exercise loop around the arena, they were all lined up at the fence. I slowed to a walk, stopping by them.

"Proceed, starting at the vertical," Mr. Braddock called out.

We took off. Well, we did everything right, though I knocked off the last rail on the hogsback, hardly clipping it with my left hind hoof. It was probably a good thing, proving I was not perfect.

Aunt Bonnie and Mrs. Albert were clapping regardless of our one fault when we came over to the fence where everyone was standing. The stony looks from the officials were hard to read. They were probably all in denial, their reasoning faculties put on overload.

Mr. Braddock left them and walked into the arena. He strode over to us and stood by my left shoulder. "If you don't mind, I'd like to take on the course with you, Jerry, just to settle a few questions I have in the back of my mind."

I felt Ann tense in the saddle and butterflies explode in my gut.

"Fine with me. I'll try to do better and give you a clean run." I looked at his boots to find he was wearing spurs. "Just remove the spurs, please."

"Oh." He looked down, but thankfully complied.

Ann dismounted, giving me a worried look as she passed him the reins.

He mounted and adjusted the lengths of the stirrups from where he sat. "Anything else I should know?"

"Though this sport is new to me, I take the same commands as any horse, and usually do not override Ann's decisions," I replied, not thrilled with his extra weight which would force me to recalculate the effort needed for every jump.

He used both his heels and the reins to turn me. "Good then. We will take this course in reverse."

That took me off guard, but I complied after Ann and Aunt Bonnie replaced the rail I knocked off on the last jump.

With him changing the course and me not being a very trusting soul after all I had been through, I expected him to pull something stupid to sabotage our efforts, but was pleasantly surprised he did not.

I made a clean run through the course, even surprising myself. When we finished, all the others were cheering along the rail, except Mrs. Stone in charge of the shows at the park.

Mr. Braddock dismounted and shook my hand saying, "That was one of the best rides I have done in my whole career. Jerry, you have a great talent befitting your equine form."

"And I got the video on your phone." Mrs. Albert held up an iPhone.

"Great. Mrs. Stone, if he would allow, you might want to see how fit he truly is for competition after a brief breather," Mr. Braddock continued.

Our eyes locked. I could almost see the distaste in hers. It was as if she was looking at something that crawled out from under a rock. "I don't need to. I have seen enough."

"Well, then, I will give you our decision by tomorrow afternoon after the board meetings," he said, patted my horse shoulder, and left the arena.

I followed as Aunt Bonnie and the rest headed up to the house, all talking in an animated manner and too far away to make anything out. Ann walked with me as I cooled down.

"What do you think?" she asked as we headed around the barn.

"Hard to say. I just hope that Mrs. Stone or Mrs. Ryder does not ruin it all. I think Mr. Braddock is cool with the idea, and he is the head of the USEF which wrote all the rules for horse shows and all from what I read on their website. But either way, we'll know by this time tomorrow," I answered.

17
The Verdict

Ann and I were rather quiet during a family dinner of pizza on our patio. I planned to stay in my centaur form rather than stress myself with constant shape shifting for jumping practice. I must admit I was feeling a bit better about being a centaur, knowing I could change at will. It was sort of like being a superhero, only this was real life and not something out of a comic book.

We were both worried about our chances of being allowed into the horse show. Through checking the show website earlier online I found it was a Class Table II, section two (a) show, and Ann in Level eight Show Jumping where the jumps would be at four feet–for the adult riders in other divisions, as well as for juniors like Ann.

This was the same format as the Grand Prix jumping with two courses that must be cleared in time allowed the second course being a jump off to find the final winner. And the monetary prize for this show was substantial at $10,000 for the top winners in the junior divisions and $50,000 in the adult. Speed and accuracy were what would count. Thus, it was a prestigious local show. Mom, Dad, and Aunt Bonnie kept casting us worried looks.

Dad finally commented, "Well, we should not ruin our digestion with worry. What will be will be, as the old saying goes. Control over our fate is an illusion."

"Thanks for the reality check, Dad," Ann said with an edge of sarcasm in her voice. "Neither of us needs a lecture on reality right now."

He frowned and was going to make another statement, but Mom cut him off with, "I wonder what Chiron would think of all this."

"He never said much, except it was nice of me to be helping Ann get to the Olympics," I answered. "And he knows how risky my getting involved and all is. Maybe you'll meet him some day. Circe didn't block him from coming into our dimension. She is one fine lady, but you don't want to cross her. Magic is as real there as science is here, and she is a master of it, manipulating the physical world with pure thought. In our dimension she'd probably be working in some government lab or teaching at a university."

Dad's eyes widened for a second. Once again, I could imagine he was thinking of somehow analyzing that world and maybe writing a paper for publication in a physics journal on travel between dimensions, regardless of how foolhardy the notion might be.

Knowing how the academic world operated on a college level with the stressful competition for research grants and lab space I had seen him go through as I grew up, I just started getting a bad feeling about it. And his next words proved my worries were not all that farfetched.

"It sure would be nice to be able to visit Chiron's dimension and do some research on the nature of other dimensions, what laws of physics apply, and the portals between them. It would make a great paper. It could even become a better way for space travel to other worlds that did not involve rockets or developing warp technology," Dad mused out loud.

"That wouldn't be a very good idea. Remember Stephen King's story *The Mist* about another dimension leaking into ours? Too much could go seriously wrong. The power structure is different and believe me, magic is real and more dangerous than you could even conceive," I warned, grabbing the last piece of pepperoni and sausage pizza. "I've been there. Remember, the myths we have of them in our world are not far off the reality."

"True, but I can just about guarantee that once this all gets out in the media, someone may try it," Dad continued.

"Not if we stay quiet about the portal and its location." I was annoyed that he might be seriously thinking of doing research on the portal with some of his students or colleagues. "Besides, Circe sealed it for all except Chiron, Mepos, Artemis, Pan, and me."

"I catch any stranger around my shed and I'm calling the police after I blast their behinds with birdshot or salt," Aunt Bonnie proclaimed, promptly shutting down that subject of conversation.

After dinner I headed off to the barn and spent most of the evening on Facebook messaging with Ben and Alice. We kicked around with more ideas for rolling up new characters, but my mind was not fully on it.

It was at the horse show jumping event and the replay of the inquisition. It was driving me crazy. I kept thinking of things I should have said or done. There was no going back, so I talked myself out of wasting my energy worrying. Tomorrow was gaming night and I'd have an answer about our inclusion in the horse show before then.

Wednesday began uneventfully. I spent the morning out in the woods trying to calm my nerves with quiet nature observation; wandering through spring blooming wildflowers, finding morels coveted by mushroom hunters, watching tent caterpillars spin their web homes in the trees, and identifying birds through song and a few sightings. I was all nice and relaxed until Ann got home from school.

Moments after I arrived to wait for her, she burst into the barn in her riding attire, crying. My heart skipped a beat. I was sure we had been refused by the USEF. "What's wrong?"

She quickly wiped her eyes with her hand, frowned and burst out, "Andrew's bitch cornered me at my locker and demanded to know why you haven't called her. I told her you were back in therapy. She would have none of it.

When I was taking my iPhone out of my locker, she grabbed it from me to call you so you wouldn't know it was her and also managed to find our jumping video before I could get it away from her with the help of Principal Archer."

"He didn't see it, did he?"

"No. Don't worry. And even if Andrea does blab, no one's going to believe her. Except maybe Andrew."

"We better hope she doesn't tell Andrew. He may be the only one who *would* believe her if he is still hot for her."

Ann shrugged. Then she took Gold Coast out of his stall and headed out of the barn for his exercise walk. When she finished, she cross tied him in the aisle, brushed him, and cleaned out his hooves with the hoof pick as I watched from my stall.

"He's still favoring that leg," she announced dismally. "I'm hoping at this point he can recover."

"We know it will be a long haul. Be patient," I said, knowing it was rather a lame statement and felt she was leading up to something.

She sighed deeply and looked over at me as she put him back in his stall. "Are you willing to be in all six shows I planned for the summer up to October if we are allowed by the USEF? A couple are out of state and . . ."

"Let's worry about that *after* we get word if we are allowed to participate in this first show of your season," I interrupted. I had visions of the whole summer turning into a media circus I really did not want, but knew it just might be inevitable.

The sound of a car stopping outside the barn brought us both to the open door as Aunt Bonnie, Mrs. Albert, and surprisingly Mr. Braddock, in a casual suit, stepped out of a black KIA Sorento. Aunt Bonnie and Mrs. Albert were doing their best to keep a poker face. They followed Mr. Braddock over to us.

He stopped a couple of yards in front of us and looked at us with a serious expression. "Good. You are both here. Let's all step into the barn, please."

We did as he asked and were quickly all standing in the aisle under the glare of fluorescent lights.

With Aunt Bonnie and Mrs. Albert standing on his right, he looked around at all of us and said, "What I have to say is best said in person rather than an impersonal e-mail or phone call. As you all know, except perhaps Jerry, the United States Equestrian Federation was founded to unite the equestrian community of competitors, leisure riders, fans, and enthusiasts all sharing a personal bond with the horse. We also honor achievement and serve as guardians of equestrian sports and provide a safe and level playing field for its equine and human athletes.

"After discussions and debates in a long joint board meeting of both the USEF and the Kentucky Horse Park this morning, it has been decided some things are bigger than sports, and in the interest of equine sports and allowing a level playing field. You will be allowed to participate in the Cross-County Hunter Jumper Horse Show at the Rolex Stadium at the Kentucky Horse Park. If that proceeds without a major problem, you will be sanctioned by the USEF to enter any and all shows you have signed up for until Gold Coast fully recovers, or is replaced by another horse."

Ann and I burst into wild cheering and I half reared, pumping the air with my right fist. The adults were all smiles. We shook Mr. Braddock's hand in turn. Ann quickly turned her handshake into a hug, taking him by complete surprise, judging by the look on his face.

He waved for silence once she let him go. "I have something else to add. Let's go out to the car." He led the way and all of us followed. "We decided to make this all official so no competitor can complain, though I doubt they will."

We stood watching as he took a large and small bag from the back of the Sorento. He handed the big one to Ann. She opened it and pulled out a saddle pad with the USEF logo on both sides. He handed the smaller bag to me. In it I found two black T-shirts with the USEF logo printed on them in white. Aunt Bonnie and Mrs. Albert were smiling and giving each other knowing looks.

"Thanks," I and Ann said in unison.

"You two have a lot of practicing to do to keep sharp and I'll leave you to it. I have some extra security measures to prepare Mrs. Ryder, and your unique substitution situation will be announced in your introduction on the PA system when you enter the arena at the show. Mrs. Ryder is giving your parents and Mrs. Albert special permission to park your horse van at the Steeplechase Barn across Nina Bonnie Boulevard from the Rolex Stadium.

"It should cut down the rubber-neckers and hopefully avert any possible disturbance when you access the exercise ring next to the stadium and stadium itself. There will be an extra security mounted officer there at your van to keep the public away and, if you wish, will escort you to the exercise ring and from there to the show arena when your class goes on."

"Craig, we will use my big four horse van with the dressing room. I will be bringing Drama Queen and am entered in the adult division. So, I will also help in keeping order," Mrs. Albert added.

Mr. Braddock nodded.

"Oh, thank you again!" Ann burst out and surprised the man with another hug.

Then, he left with Aunt Bonnie and Mrs. Albert.

Ann and I had two clear rounds of our course for practice still feeding off our victory, though technically we were sort of on probation. That evening at dinner Dad went all out with steaks on the charcoal grill on the patio and the whole family was in a festive mood.

It was nice for once not to have the horse show worry hanging over my head as heavily as it had been. Still, I knew it could become a media circus, but at this point, I felt like I could handle anything that came down the pike and the show was just a little less than three weeks away.

The *D & D* game did not quite go the way we planned. Ben, Alice, and I rolled up extra characters to play, but we did not get far with our game. Between me and Aunt Bonnie catching up on what was going on with the horse show, we all just got too excited making plans for it.

Both my friends wanted to go. We ended up concocting a crazy camp out in Mrs. Albert's big four horse trailer. After all, she said there were two extra stalls not in use, plus Dad was bringing the rented camper.

After they left to meet Alice's mom at the driveway entrance, I headed down to my hut for a well-earned sleep. Or, that was the plan.

18
Jock Vengeance

I settled into my bedding and threw the quilt over me thinking about the logistics of the show. Then my mind went into overdrive with mixed scenarios of how people would react. The thoughts turned to disjointed dreams as I drifted into sleep. Andrea was chasing me through an old growth forest on a motorcycle, firing an AR-15. Moss and chunks of tree bark sprayed everywhere. She fell into a deep hole from which the smoke poured. There was suddenly shouting and the acrid scent of wood burning. It was not in the dream.

I was jolted awake by my quilt being pulled off and the smell of goat, human sweat, and smoke.

Mepos was standing there in the darkness. "Jerry, you must come! The barn is on fire!"

I was on my feet instantly and galloped after him to the barn to find Chiron leading Drama Queen out to the pasture. One section on the side of the barn had flames creeping up from the stone foundation almost to the roof.

He instantly looked at Mepos and me approaching. "Help get the others!"

I got the hose attached to the outside spigot and turned it on, spraying the flames while shouting, "Mepos, spray the fire. I'll help Chiron!"

I handed the hose to him and ran into the barn to get Gold Coast out of his stall. Smoke had just started to drift in, and the horses left in the barn were panicking, snorting, squealing, and pacing in their stalls.

Chiron was suddenly with me, and we took the last two boarders together. Diamond was thankfully still away on the show circuit. We got them all into the pasture. Then Chiron suddenly snatched a coil of rope off the fence as he galloped past me, tying it into a loop on the run.

"Where are you going?" I shouted after him.

"After the one who did this," he yelled, heading down the driveway at a full gallop.

Far down the long drive, I glimpsed someone running toward the road. He was powerfully built and showed no signs of slowing. Off to the left, down the road about a hundred yards, I could just see a familiar parked red Ford F-150 pickup truck.

"Andrew!" I breathed and a blazing hatred blasted through me, destroying all logic. I galloped after Chiron. Peripherally, I saw the lights come on in Aunt Bonnie's house and Mepos beginning to get the fire under control, but I ignored them.

Seconds ahead of me, Chiron lassoed Andrew around his shoulders, jerking him right off his feet like a roped steer at a rodeo. I caught up to them just as

Andrew staggered to his feet, struggling to get the rope off and Chiron turning to stand a few yards away, aiming at him with a nocked arrow in his bow.

"Don't even think of moving, Andrew Collins," Chiron ordered in a vicious tone that was enough to chill anyone's blood.

"What the . . . NO-o-o-o," Andrew moaned in disbelief once he got a look at what had caught him and now had an arrow aimed at him. Frozen to the spot, he turned to look at me as I circled the both of them, my anger burning as hot as the fire. "Oh, shit! Jerry . . . you are …no …"

"Take a good look, Andrew. You called me a horse's ass, remember? Be careful what you wish for. You're going down on arson charges, you son of a bitch," I bellowed venomously, wanting to trample him to a pulp.

"I suggest we get our prisoner tied to that oak tree over there and let your authorities deal with him. Your wish for revenge and justice will both be satisfied, Jerry Swift." Chiron eased back a little on the bow string tension. His was the voice of reason that served to bring me to my senses.

Approaching sirens sounded in the distance. We got Andrew gagged with his own t-shirt and tied to the oak closer to the house and none too gently as distant flashing red and blue lights appeared around the curve in our road. We galloped back to the barn to find Aunt Bonnie in her bathrobe, her hair all frizzy, spraying the dying flames with the hose while Mepos was busy hitting at the lower flames with a wet burlap sack.

"Thank you so much, but you all better make yourselves scarce. I can handle it at this point," Aunt Bonnie said.

Chiron nodded. "Jerry, I think you better shape shift back to your human form to make this all more believable. Madam, we will meet you behind your house when this is all over and I will explain things."

"Later then, and thank you again," Aunt Bonnie said.

Chiron and Mepos disappeared into the dark as the fire trucks and a cop car came down our road paralleling Aunt Bonnie's orchard.

"I left your clothes in the barn office. They'll be a little smoky, but that will add to our story. It's safe enough to go in." Aunt Bonnie continued to spray the last of the stubborn flames.

I trotted into the smoky barn and stood by the office, wishing my human form back. I almost blacked out, but fought hard against it despite the pain. Still dizzy and in a rush, I put on my jeans without underwear and pulled my shoes on without socks.

I was a disheveled mess, but it all gave the impression I had been roused out of bed, which was a good thing. I half staggered out the barn door as the trucks pulled up and the firefighters got to work finishing the job as my parents drove up. Ann was with them. They had all thrown their jeans and shoes on, and were still partly dressed in pajamas and night gowns. Ann ran right to the barn as soon as she got out of the car.

"All the horses are safe in the pasture," I called to her. She changed direction and ran out to the pasture gate.

I was about to head after her, but was stopped by Mom who ordered, "Get checked by the EMT first."

While Aunt Bonnie and I were checked over under bright emergency lights by the EMT unit, my parents stood with us, listening to our report to the fire chief.

"It was arson," Aunt Bonnie stated as an EMT checked her heart.

"And it was Andrew Collins, our illustrious quarterback for the Greenville Stallions. I caught him running away down our drive and lassoed him. He did it. I'm sure of it. And I got the motive. His girlfriend broke up with him, and she wants to go out with me. He probably decided to get back at me by killing my sister's champion jumper recovering from an accident here in my aunt Bonnie's barn." I partly lied, but it was convincing enough. I could tell by Aunt Bonnie's shocked expression that the identity of the perpetrator had taken her by surprise as the EMTs put a blood pressure cuff on both of us.

"I'm filing charges," Dad broke in, anger showing through sleepy eyes.

"You both could have been seriously injured!" Mom cried.

"Well, I was not about to lose everything I care about," Aunt Bonnie protested.

"Neither was I," I added.

"Mrs. Foster, your BP is a little high, but that is to be expected. Drink some water and you'll be fine," Aunt Bonnie's EMT remarked.

"You're fine. Just get some water. Not soda," my EMT said. Finished, they packed up their bag and put it back in the truck. The flashing lights were turned off.

"The fire marshal will be over early in the morning to check for evidence of arson," Fire chief Michaels announced. "But I must admit, you can smell a trace of gasoline. Mrs. Foster, you were very lucky not to lose your stock or be hurt in the rescue."

"Thanks to Jerry's call and joining me. We make a good team." Aunt Bonnie squeezed my shoulder.

After making a highly edited police report with the cop that showed up after he got Andrew cuffed and into the cruiser, we were finished for the night and all of us returned to Aunt Bonnie's house as the emergency vehicles left. Aunt Bonnie put coffee on and gave me a bottle of spring water. Then I led everyone out to the back porch.

"Why are we out here?" Mom demanded.

"You'll see." I cupped my hands around my mouth and shouted, "It's okay to come out. My family knows about you and would like to meet you."

I was answered by the night breeze in the trees and the distant call of an owl. Nothing else stirred out in the darkness.

"What's all this about?" Dad started.

"My other teacher I told you about, Chiron, and a friend by the name of Mepos," I replied.

"The little goat guy? Or not so little," Ann said. "I've seen him before when that Minotaur came."

I thought I heard something. "Sh-h-h!"

The porch light caught her sour look at me. I was right. Soft hoof falls sounded in the woods. Then Chiron emerged and stepped into the light cast by the security lights.

"Good evening," he said in his resonant voice. "For those who do not know me, I am Chiron, teacher of heroes."

Everyone was staring at him in wonder.

"I think I'm in love," Ann breathed. I elbowed her gently in the ribs and she immediately elbowed me back.

"Evening," said my father.

Mom just nodded.

"Where's Mepos?" I asked.

"I sent him back. There is no need for him to be here now," Chiron replied as he walked over to the porch. "I'm here only to explain a few things, and then I will return to my own world."

Everyone went dead silent, for which I was grateful.

"I was told by one of our seers that someone was going to try to burn the barn with hopes of killing Jerry, whom he believed was residing there. Your stock was not even given a thought by him. This young man we found by the name of Andrew Collins is insanely jealous that his girlfriend left him, and is now interested in Jerry in his human form.

"However, she has recently seen those moving pictures of him in his centaur form and is even more infatuated. Because Jerry has helped us in a case for justice, and is helping his sister, a fine young mortal woman in her own right, he has become a favorite mortal to Artemis and she wishes him protected. I was sent along with Mepos to stop this crime. It pleases me that we have fulfilled our mission and all of you are safe.

"Now I must repeat a warning. The portal is only open for Jerry, Mepos, Artemis, Pan, and me. No others may pass from my dimension to yours, or from your dimension to ours. Magic is very real in my dimension and can carry over to this one. It involves the manipulation of energy in ways your science of physics has not yet discovered. It involves something I know you are familiar with here in the most rudimentary way, Dr. Swift.

"Circe is a very powerful sorceress you would not want as an enemy and Artemis is the goddess of the wild places, protector of women, and the young and must be respected. Now I will take my leave, but I will continue to teach Jerry things he will need.

"Jerry Swift and Ann, we wish you luck at your equine competitions that leads you to the much-honored

Olympics. In my dimension, we take the games seriously. Knowing the dangers in your dimension, Ann, your brother is very brave to risk all to help you attain that goal." He put his left fist to his heart. "Peace to you and yours."

With those last words, Chiron turned on his heels and trotted off to the dark woods and the old garden shed. In the porch light, I could see by the puzzled look on Dad's face that he had a ton of questions. Mom seemed fine with Chiron, as did Aunt Bonnie, and my sister had a dreamy smile on her face. We were all too tired from fighting a fire to start a major discussion of anything that happened and, after wishes of good night, headed directly to bed.

19

Clean up, Vans, and Fans

I stayed in my human form through the night, just in case the police returned for more questions. One good thing about it was sleeping back in a bed we wrestled from the guest room to my bedroom at home. Of course, I did not exactly go right to bed. After getting my undamaged iPhone and laptop out of the barn office, I called Ben and then Alice on my phone and we switched over to Facebook messenger so I could fill them in on the whole story of what happened at the barn fire.

As soon as I finished typing, Alice's response popped up with three shocked face emojis. *And Andrew saw both you and Chiron?*

I typed back. *Yep. And you know it really doesn't matter. No one will believe him if he does tell the cops. They will think he's trying to get off on an insanity plea and probably test him for drugs.*

Ben typed. *He is such a moron. I would sure like to have seen his face. ROFLMAO!!!* He followed it with three emoji faces that were laughing with tears.

Alice came back. *I hope he ends up turning rocks to sand with his new girlfriend, Bubba.*

I answered. *LOL. We'll I'm pooped. Will catch you two tomorrow or whenever.*

Ben replied. *Night.*

Alice typed. *So glad you are all right. Night.* Next to it were two emojis, praying hands and a heart.

I took a shower and totally conked out on top of my bed. Morning brought the fire marshal right after breakfast. Aunt Bonnie, Ann, and I took care of the horses while he did his inspection. The findings were, as we suspected, arson.

The accelerant was gasoline splashed on the siding. The fire had blackened half of the west side of the barn, almost all the way to the roof. We were very lucky it did not reach the hay up in the loft or the fancy chickens clear on the other side.

Aunt Bonnie planned to replace the barn siding using her insurance. The three of us were glad when the fire marshal left, taking a lot of stress and worry with him. He gave us the closure we needed.

After that drama was over, all of us agreed I should stay in my human form for a couple more days. Ann was not happy, but resting two days from training would not hurt. It was a good thing I did, too.

The local paper, Lexington Herald-Leader, sent a reporter over that afternoon, as did the local TV station, WKYT. I quickly found out barn fires are always big news in horse country, especially if it was an arson case involving show horses.

That evening when Aunt Bonnie came over for dinner, she announced she was going to sue the Collins for damages since they neglected to keep track of their delinquent son. Later in Facebook messenger I found out more juicy gossip from Ben and Alice they heard in school.

Andrew was in jail because he was considered a flight risk, and his parents refused to pay bail. I knew this new drama would play out all summer and be big community news. Meanwhile, I had to keep focused on Ann and the coming horse show.

As promised, I shapeshifted back to centaur at dawn on the third day with the same debilitating brief reaction as before. While Aunt Bonnie's barn was being repaired, I stayed out in my hut, timing practice to right after the workmen went home around three. The whole repair took only two days, so it was no big deal.

The evening of the second day, right after practice with Ann and before dinner, I was shocked to find Chiron waiting at my hut. He took a purple velvet bag out of his leather messenger bag and announced, "We are going to test you to see if you have a talent for the seer's art as some of us do. If you do have a talent for it, it will help you stay secure once news of your metamorphosis gets out in your world. If not, it's nothing to worry about. You will always have help from my world."

I was taken totally off guard by this new development, and felt my jaw drop open. Out of the velvet bag, he took a shallow silver bowl the size of a large soup bowl.

"Be careful you don't swallow a fly, Jerry Swift, and follow me down to the creek," he said with the slightest of smiles fleeting across his face.

I followed him down to the spring fed stream where he filled it. Then he held it out in both hands at a level where I could easily see the water. "What we are going to do is called scrying. Many objects can be used, like crystal balls, mirrors, or a bowl of water. Look into the water. Watch the light play on the surface. Relax. Clear your mind of all distracting thoughts. Let your eyes see images that form on the surface and shadows below. Allow yourself to drift with them; follow them deeper to find the future."

I did as he instructed. Now I have a good imagination and am open to new experiences but being science oriented, this fortune telling stuff was a little too much woo-woo, for me even with having been exposed to all this real magic, as well as reading all the *Harry Potter* books. I tried, but all I could see was a tree canopy above us and the reflection of my face and part of my chest.

"Um, I'm not doing so well. All I see is trees and me."

"Keep looking and relax," Chiron urged gently. "Listen to the stillness of the forest around you. Become part of that stillness. Empty your mind of distracting thoughts. Nothing exists but you and the water before you."

"Not easy. All I can think of is the horse show and how people are going to react to me," I said, beginning to feel frustrated. This was so much harder than archery.

At his frown, I went silent. I let myself drift, listening to the stillness of the forest. I suddenly felt a little dizzy. Briefly, I saw a crowd of people on stadium bleachers cheering a girl jumping a horse over a hogsback jump at a horse show. I could not tell who she was, only noticed that the horse was a chestnut red with a wide white blaze. Her hair was the same red color and pulled back in a bun before the vision instantly faded.

I blurted. "Oh!"

"You saw something?" he questioned and smiled.

"No big deal. Just a red-headed girl at a horse show going over a jump on a chestnut horse. I have no idea who she is. Nothing more. It made me dizzy doing that," I said. "I'm not even sure if it was my imagination or not."

He looked at me critically. "Oh, I can assure you it was not your imagination, Jerry Swift. That is Jennifer Collins and Storm Surge. She is the favorite cousin of Andrew, a highly skilled champion rider and will be your main opponent at this coming show and others. Our seers have already confirmed that vision, so yes, you have the talent.

"And before you ask, the result of the show has not been revealed. It is up to you and Ann how the stadium jumping competition ends. Not all things are revealed in scrying. There is always a free will element and what you know as chaos theory. Still, always be aware of any threat that may come to you in scrying and taking heed of it." He dumped the water and placed the bowl back in its velvet bag, and then handed it to me. "Keep this and practice when you can. You will get better with practice and don't forget that goes for your archery, too."

I took the bag, shaken by another complication rearing its head, but it was good to have a skill that provided warnings. "I'll do my best with this and my archery."

He nodded, turned, and left me standing there literally holding the bag and feeling blindsided by the revelation. I put the bowl in my messenger bag hanging on the hut wall, knowing I'd have to caution Ann about the new complication in our plans.

Dinner was a bit strange that night. Dad had gone out of town for a two-day conference and would not be joining us.

We ended up on Aunt Bonnie's back porch, pigging out on her homemade chili with corn chips from her own recipe that won the cook off last year. I told everyone about the scrying and what I had seen. Mom and Aunt Bonnie took it all in stride. Ann, however, had to make a comment.

After swallowing a mouthful of chili, she said, "I know her and always wondered if she was related to Andrew. She is such a bitch! Her big impression of herself sure makes sense now. Must be a family trait."

I could see trouble brewing. Chiron was probably right in showing me the strange world of scrying. I had to admit I learned an important lesson not to consider metaphysics as all that separate from physics. I remembered reading about a CIA program that had psychic mediums helping agents doing remote viewing of Soviet installations during the Cold War.

Ann suddenly changed the subject as she grabbed more corn chips out of the bowl on the picnic table then passed it to me. "We have to get you ready to compete."

"Well, I'm already as ready as I will ever be," I shot back, confused, and caught Aunt Bonnie and Mom's flash of grins.

Ann looked at me, dead serious. "This is a big show jumping event with hunter, jumper, and hunt seat equitation classes. Though we're in the jumper class, I want us to turn out in a more formal manner, which will give a greater impression to the judges since we are not exactly the standard horse and rider team. I will be wearing my formal turnout attire, and you will have your black USEF T-shirt and helmet on. Plus have perfect grooming, including a bath the week before, and your tail shampooed and banged and . . ."

I was so surprised I almost choked on a mouthful of chips. "Tail banged? What the . . ."

She rattled on. "No big deal. It's trimmed straight on the end. Maybe at the show I can get my friend Amy, who is a groom, to braid the top of your tail starting at the dock. That looks so neat and . . ."

"Wait! I'm not a freaking poodle!" I protested.

Mom and Aunt Bonnie broke into hysterical laughter.

When they got control, Aunt Bonnie explained, "You want to make a good impression to the judges and spectators. A spotless turnout of horse and rider shows respect to the horse, judge, and sport. It shows professionalism and it may lessen the shock you know all are going to be feeling at the event the second they see you step into the ring."

"Oh, man," I moaned and did a face palm.

All three women laughed again. I could only think of Ben, Alice, and even Chiron and Mepos laughing their asses off at how duded up I'd end up looking at the show.

It all snowballed real fast. The days passed quicker, as if time was somehow compressed. I noticed that it always seems to happen when you are not exactly looking forward to an event in life, like the first day of school or going to a dentist appointment.

At the Wednesday night *D & D* adventure, Aunt Bonnie totally mortified me by mentioning the grooming ordeal for the show since Saturday would put the show a week away. They both insisted on getting involved. I know, what are friends for?

So, I became a group project like a barn raising. My legs and fetlocks were clipped by Aunt Bonnie, getting all the stray hair. Then Ben and Alice shampooed me, each taking a side, and Ann did the same to my tail with a conditioning shampoo after brushing out every tangle. At least they used warm water.

As soon as Ann finished using her blow dryer on my tail, Aunt Bonnie trimmed my tail end hair straight at the proper height between my fetlock and hock. I was totally mortified during the whole ordeal, but thankfully they did not make snarky comments with Aunt Bonnie supervising and answering their 'how to' questions, though I knew they were just aching to roast me.

When they finished and stepped back to admire their work, Ben had to break their comparative silence with, "Are there lady centaurs in that other dimension? Cause, boy, you could get a girlfriend real fast now."

I made an instant face palm, and all laughed. The sound of a diesel engine coming up the drive thankfully ended the conversation going in that direction.

"It must be Mrs. Albert. She called last night and said since she is entered in the adult division, she'd be bringing over her four-horse van today so we could all get a head start on getting some stuff packed and not have a last-minute rush," Aunt Bonnie announced.

All of us headed to the barn door. Up the drive came the fanciest horse van I had ever seen, though I must admit I half ignored all those at the shows I went to where I watched Ann and Gold Coast compete. The whole thing was just a car length shy of the size of a tractor trailer. As Mrs. Albert pulled up next to the barn, we all went out to greet her and check out the van.

As soon as she saw me, she commented out the driver's window, "Jerry, you look fantastic! Like polished ebony."

I felt my face go hot, knew I'd blushed and barely got out, "Thanks."

"All of you have a look through the van," she continued, stepping out of the cab and opening the main ramp door. "It was a gift from my corporate lawyer husband who played the stock market frequently, and was always out to buy the very best of anything he wanted right up to the divorce. We won't talk about that now. Anyway, it's a Stainless Phoenix Coach four horse van with 2006 International 7500 crew cab Nav Star H7-750 diesel engine with six-speed automatic transmission. It has all the bells and whistles, including a high-quality Voyager camera system to help with driving and security, a front dressing room/sleeper, and for horses the stalls are adjustable to single, double, or full box stalls."

"Wow!" I exclaimed as we all stared at it as if we were looking at a UFO that had just landed.

Then we followed her in. It was extremely roomy and about as clean as a hospital room, everything scrubbed and all metal polished.

"Ben, Alice, Ann, you can use a couple of the stalls for sleeping, so bring your sleeping bags. Drama Queen and Jerry can have the other two. I'll take the bed in the dressing room," Mrs. Albert said.

"I won't be camping," Aunt Bonnie spoke up. "I'll be making day trips to watch the stadium jumping. After all, I have stock to care for, remember?"

"Mom and Dad will bring our camper. Dad got a good spot in the park campground within easy walking distance to Rolex Stadium. He's bringing the grill, so that means hot dogs and hamburgers on Saturday night. Mom's taking time off from real estate. Besides wanting to keep an eye on security, they don't want to miss this," Ann said.

"Oh, because of our situation, as planned we have special permission to park by the Steeplechase Barn right across Nina Bonnie Boulevard from the stadium. Mr. Stewart himself will be meeting us there with an extra security guard. Just talked to him before I left the house. We are all trying our best not to cause too much of a stir, but be prepared for a media circus," Mrs. Albert cautioned us. "You have to be checked by a vet before competition, and he will come to the van rather than you going to him and waiting your turn with the other competitors as usual. All he does is check your health papers and make you trot up and down to check for lameness. That will be done down the aisle inside the Steeplechase Barn out of sight of the public. They will have the building clear of grooms, and it will be done after we arrive on Friday afternoon."

"He will be in for a shock," I cracked. "And blow our plan of avoiding a media circus as long as we can."

"Not if he wants to keep his job at the park," Mrs. Albert came back. "We will not be able to prevent a media circus anyway, so let's just face that fact now. We can only hold it off as long as possible."

"I have been warning about that all along, but I still intend to see this to the end." I looked over at Ann, who caught my glance.

After everyone finished checking out the van, they packed some of the items we would need, like extra brushes and all. Ben and Alice would bring what they needed on Friday and pack it in with all the tack and last-minute stuff Ann and Mrs. Albert would be adding.

Uneasiness grew cold in my gut. That night, I decided to work on my scrying and brought the bowl to the barn in my messenger bag. Ann and Aunt Bonnie insisted I bunk there so I would stay clean instead of picking up forest debris out sleeping at my hut or wandering the woods the way I liked to do when I got bored. But thankfully, they left me alone after dinner.

Well, I made a huge effort that seemed to last for hours, trying to clear my mind to peer into the future. All I got was a one second glimpse of a crowd of people up on stadium bleachers staring back and the flash of cameras and iPhones. I could make nothing of it and quit for the night.

20
Prelude

Well, the last week before our departure for the Kentucky Horse Park seemed to fly by. Practice became more intense. My mind went into overdrive as usual, and I developed a case of nerves that amounted to stage fright in the worse way. I gave up trying to ease my worries by scrying. I could not empty my mind to relax enough to get it to work. This was probably all a throwback to the constant harassment from jock types most of my life.

While everyone was doing the final packing of the van after lunch on our day of departure, I just watched, standing by the van in one of my new black USEF T-shirts. All knew I was worried. Ann, Alice, and Ben insisted on saying something encouraging every time they passed me going up the ramp to hand Mrs. Albert an item she packed in its proper place.

"You got this," Alice said, bringing a box of grooming tools for Drama Queen.

"You can do it. Just put your mind to it." Ben carried Drama Queen's saddle, bridle, and breast plate into the trailer.

"You're the best!" Ann chimed in, bringing mine.

Before we left, Ann gave me a quick brushing to make my coat nice and shiny. Then we were off for the Kentucky Horse Park, which was only forty-five minutes away.

I had not been there since an eighth-grade field trip, yet remembered a lot about it, plus refreshing my mind the night before by a visit to their website had helped. Basically it is a working horse farm and an educational theme park opened in 1978 in Lexington, Kentucky dedicated to man's relationship with the horse.

It covers 1,224 acres and has everything from the International Museum of the Horse and shows facilities in the Rolex Stadium and Alltech Arena, to racetracks, a home for some of the world's greatest retired competition horses from the racing industry, and a beautiful campground for visitors. Complete with a swimming pool and convenience store.

Ann always called it "the Disneyland for horse people" and that was a great description. I was not all that into it when I last visited and wished now that I had paid more attention. But I could say that I had a closer relation to the horse than anyone who would be there.

I watched out the small window near my box stall in the van and caught some of the verdant late spring scenery as we went down the highway. My only company was Drama Queen for Ann, Ben, and Alice were all in the cab with Mrs. Albert. Luckily, the cab had a back seat.

Drama Queen was a perfect roommate. She was calm as an old plow horse. I knew we had arrived when I saw the statue of Man o' War in the memorial garden at the entrance through my narrow window.

But we did not go to the main entrance to the parking lot. We headed down Cigar Lane, past Race Track Road and Big Barn Road, turned down Nina Bonnie Boulevard, and past the Show Office to pull in at the Steeplechase Barn across from Rolex Stadium. When I checked my watch, it was 3:15 p.m.

It was a long time since the engine cut off that I heard someone enter via the regular door into the horse section of the van. I turned my human torso to look. It was Mrs. Albert and the rest were right behind her.

"You okay back here?" she asked cheerily.

"We're fine. Nice smooth ride." I forced a grin. I was not all that happy knowing I'd have my freedom drastically curtailed because of my situation and the need to not stir the pot and attract unwanted attention so early.

"I was on the phone with Mrs. Stone. The vet will be here in about ten minutes. They are not waiting until it gets dark like we originally wanted. He has a busy schedule with this show. Mr. Steward will be here any minute with one of his security officers. They will clear personnel from the Steeplechase Barn so you can have your vet inspection with Drama Queen."

"I sure hope the vet stays cool," I said.

"So do I," Alice agreed.

"Count me in on that, too," Ann put in, and about killed what little confidence I was trying to cultivate at that moment.

I heard an electric golf cart pull up. That had to be security. Mrs. Albert left us immediately. She started talking with whoever it was, and I could not make out any of the words as Ann, Alice, and Ben lined up protectively along my portable stall rails with determined looks on their faces like seasoned warriors. Ben reached over and grabbed a pitchfork off its wall hook as if on a second thought.

"Ah, guys, you know word of my existence is going to get out, so we all might as well start accepting that fact and chill," I urged.

They all turned their heads to look at me in a resolute manner.

"No matter what happens, we got your back, man," Ben announced.

"Guess we are sort of overreacting a little." Alice lost her Viking warrior queen stance.

"A little?" I returned, pointing to the pitchfork in Ben's hands.

He shrugged and looked totally self-conscious. We all had a brief snicker over it as he hung up the pitchfork.

Suddenly, the ramp door opened, and Mrs. Albert came in.

"Dr. Fergus will be here in a moment, and I'm starting with Drama Queen, so Mr. Stewart and I have a moment to put him at ease. You three can come out with Jerry when we're ready." She took Drama Queen from her stall across from us and grabbed two manila envelopes with our health papers from a folder holder on the wall near the ramp on her way out. "Keep your fingers crossed."

The two of them went down the ramp as we heard another golf cart pull up.

As soon as the electric motor cut off, a loud gruff voice complained, "You know this is all highly irregular and if it was not on the insistence of Mr. Braddock, I would never have allowed this interruption to my very busy inspection schedule. Now, if you will, let's go in the barn and get this over with. You said two horses. Where is the other?"

"He will be with us in a moment," Mrs. Albert said, sounding further away.

The conversation quickly became muffled by distance.

"I don't like him," Alice spoke up.

"Neither do I," Ann added.

Ben just frowned.

"We have no choice." I shrugged.

While I waited, I felt as if my stomach was full of butterflies chased by grasshoppers until Mrs. Albert came back with Drama Queen. She put the mare back in her stall. "Come on, gang. Dr. Fergus is waiting for us."

"Did you tell him about me?" I asked.

"Yes, and I think he believed it was a practical joke until I showed him the short video on my phone and your papers, plus a note from Mr. Braddock who was kind enough to send an official permission to enter from the USEF in case we had a problem. Now Dr. Fergus is quite anxious." She flashed a grin.

Escorted by my sister and friends crowding around me, we all headed into the big Steeplechase Barn where Dr. Fergus stood holding a clipboard with Mr. Stewart right next to him and one of his security guards.

Both Dr. Fergus and the security guard stared at me as if they were looking at a ghost. It was a complex look of fear mixed with awe and a sprinkle of denial.

"Jerry, this is Dr. Fergus and he will be checking you for any lameness," Mrs. Albert said as we approached.

"And this is Mike Andrews who will be your added security," Mr. Stewart stated.

I held out my hand to Dr. Fergus. "Hello, doctor. Unlike your other patients, I don't bite or kick." I know it was lame, no pun intended, but I had to say something to quiet the fear or outrage I could feel around him. I noticed the two envelopes of our health papers on his clipboard.

His eyes grew wide and he slowly grasped my hand. "Remarkable. And you feel okay with . . . with . . ."

"The curse took some getting used to, but I'm doing fine. I'm helping my sister by substituting for her injured horse that was entered. We have been working very hard." I could see him relax as a slow smile spread across his face.

Then Mike stepped forward and shook my hand. "You have no idea how just plain weird this is. Like I walked into a *Harry Potter* movie or something. No offense."

"No offense taken. I'm a science geek in the intellectually gifted classes hoping for a career in Cosmology and have been treated like I was weird all my life anyway," I returned.

"Well, you can count on me doing my job," Mike assured. "I have a horse lined up so I can keep up with you and your sister when you go to the exercise ring before your class and will stick close and escort you to the arena and back when it's time."

"Thanks." I saw Ann was beaming.

"The thanks should go to my boss. I'm just a peon," Mike joked as Mr. Stewart clapped him on his shoulder.

"Well, let's get you checked out, Chiron's Pride." Dr. Fergus passed the envelopes back to Mrs. Albert. "Trot on down halfway in the barn, then turn and come back at a trot straight at me."

I nodded and did as asked.

"Perfect. Perfect. Mrs. Albert, both entrees are passed and all health papers are in order," Dr. Fergus remarked, writing notes on his clipboard. "Good luck to you both."

"Thanks," Ann said.

"Thanks," I echoed.

"Well, I'll leave you in Mike's capable hands. I'll probably see you again before the weekend is over. Good luck to all of you." Mr. Stewart got into the golf cart with

Dr. Fergus and drove off down the road towards the show office.

"Boy, am I glad that's over with," Ann broke our silence.

"You and the rest of us," I agreed. "Guess I better get back into the van. The grooms probably need to get back to work." I walked towards the van ramp.

"I'll give them the all clear, and then I'm going for my iced tea in my golf cart," Mike said and got on his two-way radio to the barn manager.

"And speaking of grooms," Ann broke in, catching up to me as I ducked and stepped into the van. "Amy should be here any moment to braid your and Drama Queen's tails."

"What?" I cried, stopping short and turning to face her.

"Don't you remember I told you just the other day I wanted us to go in formal to make a good impression?" Ann shot back.

"But what will she . . ." I started to protest, but she cut me off.

"It's all fine. She is cool with it and won't tell anyone. I think she thinks I'm playing a trick on her."

Mrs. Albert walked over and stopped with Ben and Alice at the bottom of the ramp. "I got a cooler stuffed with soda in the back. Let's take a well-earned break while we wait."

The words were no sooner out of Mrs. Albert's mouth when we heard another golf cart approaching and Mike jogged over.

"Are you expecting company?" he asked.

"It's Amy Winter. She is a groom from the Hunter Jumper Barn and she is going to do some tail braiding," Ann assured him. "She is okay with our secret."

Mike nodded and stood by, drinking his iced tea. Amy pulled up next to the van, staring at everyone. I backed further into the van so I would not be seen. But I did get a quick glimpse of her. She had to be about twenty or so and was quite good looking, her long brown hair in a kind of thick braid that goes up the back of one's head.

"Well, where are they?" I heard her say cheerfully.

"Do Drama Queen first. I want to see what it looks like before I agree to this," I whispered as loud as I dared at Ann at the ramp entrance. I did not want to look like a fool, which was probably a stupid notion.

"Was that him? He's real?" Amy's voice sounded along with her feet coming up the ramp.

I froze. There was no place to hide.

Ann giggled. "Yes. Jerry, it's okay."

Suddenly Amy was in the van standing a couple of yards in front of me and staring wide eyed. "Oh. My. God. He is so awesome!"

"Er-r-r," was all I said, wishing I had a place to hide despite what Ann said.

Amy bubbled on with a dreamy look in her eyes. "He would make the perfect understanding boyfriend to any girl on the show circuit. Oops, I should not have said that. Have you even thought of what you two could do? You could probably easily get an exhibition riding job here tomorrow. God, maybe get into eventing and get into the Olympics only a few years down the line. Alls you two would have to learn is dressage . . ."

"Or end up in a lab being dissected," Alice snapped defensively, and stepped between us.

"All right," Mrs. Albert interjected. "Amy, let me bring out Drama Queen so you can get started and Jerry, you can watch from the safety of the van. It does end up looking very nice."

I could have kissed Mrs. Albert for derailing Amy's train of thought, and wondered if Alice was showing a hint of jealousy by her protective behavior. I hoped Amy's comments did not give Ann any ideas.

It was bad enough my mind suddenly jumped to the possibility that the same thought had crossed Mr. Braddock's mind and maybe some others. I still wanted a career in Cosmology and not equestrian sports. My ace in the hole was the ring that allowed me to change back. I hoped Ann would not mention that, and I promised myself to corner her on that later.

Well, I spent the next half hour watching the complex process of brushing and braiding a tail from where it joined the body at the dock and went about halfway, leaving the rest of the tail free and looking like a long fly switch. It was sort of cool looking, so I agreed to let Amy do mine in the van under the lights.

The bad thing was she kept on and on how lucky Ann was and how we could make tons of money going to Grand Prix events and other schemes. She forgot herself several times and lovingly patted my butt like you would a regular horse. It was embarrassing and I protested every time she did it. I was not sad to see her leave. And I don't think Alice was, either, having watched her like the proverbial hawk every second she worked and scowled like a wet cat every time Amy patted my butt.

Ann left for a half hour to walk the jumping course with the judges and other riders. When she came back, she looked at me, shrugged, frowned, and commented, "It's a freaking pile of spaghetti with ten jumps. Number one is vertical. We head off diagonally toward the right between jumps seven and eight to number two, a triple spread.

"Then go off to the left between three and four, skirting number ten close as possible to save time, and keep looping left for a good run at the triple combination at three and double spread at four. Next, go right to detour around eight to take on five, which is a wall and six, which is a descending oxer. Afterward, it's a sharp right to take number seven, an ascending oxer and sort of loop left to number eight, which is a hogsback.

"Finally, off to the left for number nine, which is a Liverpool, and last number ten, which is a double spread and finish. The jump off will be a selection of eight of those jumps in a different order for less time. They are all decorated real fancy with flowers and hedges with many of the rails painted in colorful stripes. It's very distracting. You'll see it all tomorrow."

Sure, the thought briefly hit that I could shape shift back to my human form and creep up in the dead of night to check it all out, but that would be stupid, especially with all the security. Though I was not feeling all that optimistic, I came back with, "We got this, Ann."

When my parents arrived later around 7 p.m., everyone went to dinner but me. I shared a couple of pizzas and liters of soda with Mike in the van, and he had to know the story behind the curse. I, of course, told him a heavily edited version, ending with a big lie about not finding the stone yet.

He went off on his rounds before going home for the night when Ann and everyone returned. With a need for an early start for the next day since Ann's class was on at 10 a.m., we all turned in early with a case of show jitters.

21
Big Day and Big Trouble

I was awakened around 5:00 a.m. by grooms going about their business in the barn and Drama Queen nickering at Mrs. Albert who showed up in boots, jeans, and a USEF t-shirt to start her pre-show chores. Ann was not far behind. Ben was still snoring, with Alice asleep out in their stalls. Ann and Mrs. Albert took it upon themselves to be the alarm clock.

Ann dropped a bucket and got a dirty look from Drama Queen while Mrs. Albert clapped her hands. "Up and at 'em. You're burning daylight."

They both got up, stumbling around like a couple of zombies. Then they went off to the restrooms in the barn to freshen up with our laughter shadowing them.

It was a perfect late spring day for a show sunny and due to be in the low 70s. Mom and Dad showed up around 6:00 a.m. with McDonalds breakfasts for everyone. Right after breakfast, Ann got busy checking my tack and safety equipment. She, Ben, and Alice got at my last-minute grooming with Mom and Dad watching, strangely silent.

Two new bits of grooming were added. My white socks were baby powdered and brushed with a soft brush to make them snow white, and my hooves were slathered with hoof dressing to give them a clean shine before the boots, and all were put on.

I was sprayed with coat dressing, rubbed down with a towel, and brushed out to a nice sheen. Of course, I washed up, brushed my hair and teeth and put on a fresh black USEF T-shirt.

Mom and Dad went off through a growing crowd of riders and spectators, moving along the road to the exercise ring that was alongside the Rolex Stadium to wait for us.

"Ann, you better get dressed," Mrs. Albert said.

Ann went off to the van dressing room to change from her stable clothes to her formal riding habit while Mrs. Albert, Alice, and Ben helped get my tack on. We were supposed to be in the exercise ring by 9:30 a.m. with both of us due to make our class at 10:00 a.m. All junior and young rider classes would be run on Saturday, including Jumper, Hunter, and Hunter Equitation with adult classes on Sunday.

According to the program I was reading while I waited, there were twenty contenders due to compete in Ann's Jumper class. Jennifer Collins and Storm Surge were among them. The more I peeked out over Ben and Alice's heads at the increasing number of horses and riders passing along the road to the stadium, the more nervous I became.

But I had made a promise to stand in for Gold Coast and no matter what, I was determined to keep it. I touched my ring absentmindedly and wondered if Chiron's seers were watching it all or perhaps even him.

"Looks like they will reach the estimated number of spectators," Alice commented.

"And then some," Ben added.

They both seemed to enjoy their horse and people watching.

Mike arrived at 9:00 a.m. sharp and called from outside, "Hello. Good morning."

When I peeked out over the ramp, I saw he was in his security uniform with a radio on his belt, plus a hunter orange vest for visibility, and mounted on a dark bay gelding.

"Good morning. Just waiting for Ann," I called and waved along with Alice and Ben from the top of the ramp.

Mrs. Albert and Ann came walking around from the dressing room on the other side of the van. Though I'd seen Ann in her more formal attire for competition before, she looked particularly good this time and I hoped that exchange student from England she was so infatuated with from school, Robert Dickerson, did not show up to watch her as he had promised.

Yet, I figured the sight of me might give him pause. Her riding breeches were white and tucked into tall black boots. A white rat catcher-style shirt with choker was worn under a black coat. On her head was the required riding helmet in black. We would be a flashy formal study in black and white.

Then Mike said, "Let's get going."

I walked down the ramp with Alice and Ben taking pictures with their phones. At the bottom, Ann climbed into the saddle. No one around us reacted immediately, all in their own horsey worlds. Mr. Braddock drove up to us in a golf cart.

"You two look great," he remarked. "Oh, I wanted to let you know in an effort to head off possible trouble, each show program is having a short notice about your unique circumstances stapled into it when it is handed out. The note states you are sanctioned to enter, having passed all tests and been given permission by the USEF, show chairman, and park. It was on the insistence of the park CEO and show chairman.

"There will be a further announcement in your introduction, as you were probably expecting. We are seeing to it that no media disturbs you before or during your class. So far, I do know WKYT and RIDETV are here to film a little of the show for sports news. We want to keep the playing field level as in all our sanctioned events. Mr. Andrews, you call back up and have a show steward call me and your boss if anyone tries to cause serious trouble. The stewards will all be wearing red coats, as usual."

"Thanks," Ann said.

"Thanks," I echoed and half mumbled to myself under my breath, "I knew something like this would happen."

"Good luck, you two. And, Jerry, stop worrying and do your best. I know you are capable of great things." He drove off.

All of us headed down Nina Bonnie Boulevard to the entrance of the exercise ring by the stadium with Mike in the lead. As I was afraid, heads started to turn with people pointing at our little parade and looking with various expressions of disbelief and a few frowns from some riders, most of which were high school or college age. One of the young male riders on a dark bay gelding yelled, "What is this? A circus?"

A woman standing next to him added, "Can we expect unicorns?"

And a portly middle-aged man in a flowery Hawaiian shirt next to her complained, "They're doing anything now to increase show attendance numbers."

Another young male rider on a gray gelding yelled back, "Brody, shut the fuck up! Check the program. They are sanctioned by the USEF, and that's fine with me."

I felt Ann stiffen up. I forced a smile and waved at a few and was quite surprised to get smiles and waves back, including the rider on the gray. In moments, we were at the exercise ring with quite a few people following us on foot and horseback.

"Are you real?" a man who was on foot with a teenage girl running next to him yelled from behind us.

"You bet!" I turned to yell back as Ann just nodded and smiled nervously.

"Keep walking," Mike called over his shoulder as he stopped at the exercise ring gate while a wide-eyed attendant opened it.

Those who were following on foot as if I was a rock star or space alien spread out along the fence. My eyes fell on Jennifer on the other side of the ring, trotting toward us on Storm Surge. Trouble. As she drew closer, I could see she was frowning.

As soon as she was within hearing distance, she shouted in a surprisingly strong voice that must have also been a Collins trait, "How dare you bring that freak onto these grounds!"

She stopped her horse, making sure she blocked our way into the ring. Her blue eyes were like ice.

"I'll have to ask you to move," Mike commanded.

"Or what?" she snapped. "I'm making a formal complaint to the steward. My dad's a lawyer and will make it stick."

"Was he your barn burning cousin's lawyer?" I retorted, letting everyone know I was by no means mute or a dumb beastly creature and certainly would not cower to a bully.

"Get out of the way," a slim middle-aged man with hair just starting to go gray hollered, circling around the crowd at the fence. I noticed he was dressed in a riding habit with a name badge on his jacket.

Ann spoke to me in a low voice. "Oh, my God! That's Alexander Vance, an Olympic gold medalist and one of the judges I was with last night when riders walked the course."

Jennifer was about to say something to him, but stopped, turned Storm Surge away none too gently, and trotted off to the other side of the ring. There, a couple of rail practice jumps were set up, one at about two feet and one at about four feet for part of our exercise. She cantered Storm Surge at the four foot one and sailed over it as if to challenge us and distract attention from the crowd.

I followed Mike into the ring, and he stayed by the gate while I continued watching and half mumbled, "Who does that bitch think she is?"

"She's always been mouthy at the competitions where I've seen her," Ann answered. "Let's get warmed up and stay away from her. We're due to go last. She's on first and that will be hard since she will not see how everyone else takes on the course to make any change of plans for herself."

"Well, I'm all for taking that jump after a brief trot around the ring to let the bitch know we are just as much a force to be reckoned with as anyone else here. And like Mr. Braddock said the other day, 'Some things are bigger than sports'."

"You're on!"

We did just that and even got some applause from some of the people who had followed us to the exercise ring. Many of them shot photos with cameras and phones. We both knew Jennifer saw us.

She gave us a black look when we cantered past her. We were glad we had some supporters. It was at that moment I realized some horse people liked underdogs.

Well, things got really interesting from that point on. I had to remind myself this was basically a speed trial, and one had to race through the jumps as safely and as fast as possible while avoiding any knock downs. Because of the length of the course, we had sixty-five seconds to get through, otherwise we'd have a point added for each second over that time.

Every rail knocked down would cost four faults that would be added to the time. Any refusal would cost four faults, a second refusal caused elimination as did a fall, and failure to cross the starting line before the timer started within forty-five seconds no score would result. Being last in the class, we both decided to wait as long as possible to line up with the others at the entrance to the show arena to avoid any more negative confrontations.

We could see all that went on in the arena by way of the thirty-three by eighteen-foot full range Daktronics LCD video display board mounted high over the arena, plus we could hear the announcer's comments on everything over the PA system. Neither of us was in a mood for anymore altercations, though most of the horse people seemed like good sports and left us alone while we exercised to warm up. We both knew all too well how strange we appeared and the reputation centaurs of myth had with those knowledgeable in that area of literature.

We stopped our exercise to watch Jennifer as soon as the subject matter on the PA system jumped from a short rehash of her just so wonderful record to the bell that announced the run up to her start. Watching her on the video display, I instantly noticed the jumps were far more ornate than ours at home. The Liverpool jumps even had a riverboat attached and some of the upright standards that held the rails looked like the towers at Churchill Downs of Kentucky Derby fame, and other jumps even looked like stone walls and country bridges. It would be very distracting. Jennifer had a perfect round and was all self-congratulatory smiles with a fast time of 53.02. Her family and friends were going wild in the stands.

The turns of the others blew by as we got in a little more exercise before we left with Mike to get behind the last entry before we were to go on, thankfully a whiteboard fence kept spectators back off the walkway. None beat Jennifer's time so far and the one that did, a rider by the name of Allen West on a mare called Sprite, ended up with one fault from knocking down the top bar of the last fence that added four seconds to his time for a total of 55.01.

Ahead of us was John Byrd, who I remember from the program, on a dapple-gray gelding called Glacier Bay. He was the same guy who stood up for us against that Brody character, and he looked over at us as Mike fell back at the walkway gate from the exercise arena. I was really thankful Mike's presence seemed to keep the curious back.

The steward at the open arena gate called, "John Byrd and Glacier Bay."

Ann cheerily called to John, "Good luck!"

I smiled as his stats were announced on the PA along with a brief mention that he had rescued Glacier Bay from an abusive situation, and had worked with him for five years to make him a top contender.

John nodded, smiling back as he trotted Glacier Bay into the arena, then cantered off to start when the bell sounded. We watched him make a clear run, but he lost time on a few wide turns, ending with 54.00.

The steward called, "Ann Swift and Chiron's Pride."

When John passed us on his way out of the arena, he smiled. "Good luck to you both."

I was so distracted by a case of the gut butterflies when the whole stadium crowd gasped as if one entity at our appearance at the entrance that I only half heard the quick blurb on Ann and mention of the unusual, but sanctioned, substitute for her regular mount of her brother registered as Chiron's Pride, a victim of a curse. The bell rang, signaling us to head for the start that was marked by a red and a white flag.

I hesitated, but Ann dug her heels into my ribs to get me out of my fog. "A little red and a white flag on all the jumps mark the direction you go. Red is always on the right. I know the order from the walk-through last night."

"Why didn't you tell me about the little flags before?" I questioned.

"It slipped my mind," she returned.

"I hope nothing else has," I shot back, and hopped forward at a trot and the second I entered the arena heading for the start, an audible collective gasp sounded from more of the spectators. I estimated the crowd in the stands and along the fences to be at least three thousand. The spectators went eerily silent. There was a sudden flurry of flashes from a multitude of cameras.

"Let's go, steady canter," Ann tapped my ribs again with her heels.

I picked up my pace, charged past the start flags, the timer started, and I took the first jump, a vertical with no problem.

Boo's sounded from the seats of Jennifer's family and supporters and from a couple of other spots in the stands.

"Go right between jumps seven and eight for number two, the triple spread," Ann directed.

We headed off even faster diagonally toward the right between jumps seven and eight to number two, a triple spread with striped rails and lots of flowers. I flew over it with inches to spare. From the silence came a few weak cheers, clapping, and more camera flashes.

"Go between three and four and bear left to number ten, and double back to take three and four head on. Pick up the pace if you can. We got to beat Jennifer's time, and this is the place to do it," Ann instructed.

I kept up the speedy canter, going off to the left between three and four, skirting number ten extremely close to save time, kept left for a good run at the triple combination at number three each between Churchill Downs spires, and double spread at number four that looked like a suspension bridge.

There was only one stride between the triple combination fences, and I had to adjust my speed. Then I picked up momentum for number four. I felt my hind left boot touch the top rail of number four's second fence of the double spread.

My breath caught in my throat. The rail wobbled, but it did not go down. There were more scattered cheers and clapping.

"Go around right around eight, the hogsback to take the wall at five." Ann signaled with the reins.

I went right to detouring close around number eight to take on five, which was a faux stone wall, and six within a few strides, which was a descending oxer striped, red, white and blue. I cleared it without issue to even more cheering.

"Watch this sharp turn backtracking to seven and veer a little left for eight," Ann said.

My loop back was safe but sharp to take number seven, an ascending oxer and I veered my course slightly left to fly over number eight, which was a hogsback with vines and big sunflowers covering the standard supports holding the rails. Clapping and louder cheers with camera flashes followed us.

"Loop to the left on the outside for nine and ten." Ann again signaled with the reins and her heels.

"I got this," I said, finally feeling better about this whole challenge and greatly encouraged by more supporters than I ever dreamed of siding with us.

I headed for the crazy river boat jump number nine, which was a Liverpool, and got over that, just barely making it past the water's edge where my back hooves hit the ground. I surged ahead for the last jump, number ten which was a double spread between gold horse heads. I sailed over it and blasted past the finish with Ann gently hauling back on the reins to applause and cheering from almost half the stadium.

"We're done," she announced as I slowed to a trot, then a walk.

We both glanced up at the clock on the big video screen. Our time was 52.05. We had beaten Jennifer's time for the number one slot. Ann shrieked and grabbed me around my human chest and back under my arms in a hug while I grinned from ear to ear and pumped my right fist into the air in a celebration of a hard-won victory considering this was the first athletic competition of my life and I had not made an ass of myself.

But that was not the end. There would be a jump off next for what turned out to be the six of us without faults from this first round as soon as the arena crew could rearrange the jumps. It would be a shorter course. No one got to see and walk ahead of time, and we would all go in reverse order highest time first with less time to do it. First round times would be carried over. And most importantly, anything could happen.

22
Jump Off

While we waited for the arena crew to set the jump off course, the six of us hung out in the exercise ring or in the short walkway from the exercise ring to the arena. Mike stayed right with Ann and me.

In order of our first-round finishing times from highest to lowest up on the video screen that would be our starting order of our next runs in the jump off round our group list included Charlie Gibbons and Truant, Sally Reese and Resolve, Wendy Potts and Darling Lily, John Byrd and Glacier Bay, dear Jennifer Collins and Storm Surge and us last.

Just as expected, Jennifer walked Storm Surge over to us for some trash talk the second John came over smiling pleasantly and about to say something.

Jennifer cut John off with a savage, "Who's going to join me in filing a complaint about this freak being allowed in this show?"

Wendy and Sally walked their horses away while Charlie gave her a look of daggers from where he sat his horse by the arena entrance.

"Why don't you just take a chill pill? Jerry's all horse where it counts," John shot back, frowning at her.

My body suddenly decided I had to go, and I was no longer embarrassed about doing it in public. "I can prove that right now." The words were no sooner out of my mouth than I raised my tail and dropped a steaming pile of manure. "Excuse me. A perfect editorial comment to your bigotry and bullying."

Several people within an easy ear shot who had been watching and listening to us started laughing, and John and Mike were among them. As soon as Mike got control, he put his hand on his radio and warned, "If you don't stop the harassment, Miss Collins, I'm calling the steward, my boss, and Mr. Braddock and you may just find yourself disqualified for poor sportsmanship."

"This is not over," she snapped and rode away to a middle-aged couple by the fence in the exercise arena that I assumed were her parents.

"Bitch!" Ann called, determined to get a last word in.

"Jerry, I can't believe you did that." John was still snickering.

"There are a few advantages to having a horse body," I said and he laughed even harder.

By the time that drama was done, a steward came over. "Ladies and gentlemen, the new start is at the first-round finish with jump number ten. Two have been pulled, the triple spread at three and the Liverpool at nine. There are eight jumps and you have 50.2 seconds to finish. Good luck to you."

The alarm bell rang to start the next round. Charlie and on his brown gelding, Truant cantered out and we all watched from the gate. We glanced at the big screen as he rode once around the outside of the course for a quick look and went to start at the old number ten.

He was making quick time until he guided Truant over the wall. Truant clipped the wall with his right front hoof and one of the stone painted boxes fell, causing him to stumble upon landing. But he regained his footing quickly and made it over the last fence, a single vertical. His time of 45.03 was penalized to 49.03. I did not miss the satisfied smirk on Jennifer's face.

"Sally Reese and Resolve," the steward called.

Sally rode into the ring on her gray, did a quick ride around the course and headed directly for the double spread, turning a bit wide to begin. By the time she finished it was a clear run, but no record breaker at 50.00.

"Wendy Pots and Darling Lily," the steward called.

After her quick ride around the course on her sorrel mare, Wendy used the same strategy, starting with a wide turn for her canter at the first jump. Over the course Darling Lily seemed to be distracted and, on both oxers, she hard rubbed rails with her hind hooves and was very lucky they did not fall. Her clear run went one and a half seconds overtime for a total of a disappointing 51.05.

"John Byrd and Glacier Bay," the steward called.

Of all left in our class, if I had to choose someone to win this round, it would be him if not Ann and me. After their circuit ride around the course, John and

Glacier Bay did not make as wide a turn as the others before him to take the first jump and shaved off some time. Glacier Bay flew over the jumps, never coming close to rubbing any rails. To cheering from the crowd, they finished clear with the best time yet of 47.02. Ann and I joined in with the spectators clapping for him as he left the arena. His would be the time to beat.

"Way to go," I said to him as he passed us.

He grinned and, in passing at a walk, leaned over and playfully clapped my human shoulder. I caught Jennifer's stony look as the steward called, "Jennifer Collins and Storm Surge."

She trotted past us with the words, "You are going down and your freak friend, too, John."

Jennifer and Storm Surge trotted into the arena and immediately broke into a swift canter around the course and up the center to check the course layout when the bell rang. Turning sharply at the same speed, they passed the starting line to take the double spread as if it was just a low garden fence. They powered on in perfect synch over the triple combination and the other jumps and finished clear, beating John with a time of 46.03.

As they left the arena to cheer and passed us, she smirked. "You and your freak try beating that without knocking off a rail."

I frowned, but said to Ann before she could answer, "Don't give her the satisfaction of a response. We'll just make her swallow her hubris and watch her choke on it.

Watching over the screen up there I've got the course memorized. Let's go for speed."

"Ann Swift and Chiron's Pride," the steward called.

We trotted into the arena to the surprise of more than half the spectators cheering. We cantered around the course like the others, so we'd hear no complaints. All went quiet as I switched to a speedier canter and streaked across the starting line for the double spread first jump and cleared it with inches to spare and Ann in perfect form.

My brain went into overdrive, calculating our course to the nearest inch to slice fractions off our time and making the sharpest turns where I could. I was tired of being considered a freak in my world because of being a genius and now a centaur. I was tired of bullies and bigots. Determination to make fools of all of them melted doubt.

With Ann signaling with reins and legs, our timing was perfect for the triple combination and following double spread. I made a sharper right for the hogsback than Jennifer had and powered over it, making a sharp right again for the double oxer. I swung in a tight loop to the left for the ascending oxer and cleared it.

The wall loomed ahead and I poured on speed, feeling Ann's legs grip tighter. I pushed myself hard to get over it, clearing it and charged for the last fence, the simple vertical. I jumped it, but heard and felt my left hind hoof boot rub it slightly. The top rail wobbled precariously on the standards as my hooves hit the ground.

Many in the crowd gasped. It did not fall. Cheering sounded as we slowed down and looked up at the video display with a time of 45.05. Ann hugged me again as we headed for the arena gate. The steward even gave us the thumbs up sign and smiled. I smiled back; glad it was over.

All of the jump off contenders were waiting for us beyond the gate. Jennifer hung back.

"Great going, guys." John reached out to shake our hands.

"Yeah. That was just strange." Sally shook Ann's hand, then shyly took mine.

"Now what? We're finished, right?" I asked almost hopefully as I caught sight of Mike at the exercise arena gate.

"No, don't forget we go back in for our ribbons and other awards starting with sixth place," Charlie replied.

"Which will be me," Wendy stated, patting Darling Lily's neck.

"And a victory lap," Ann added. "Don't you remember from watching my shows?"

"I usually missed that part and was heading to the concessions for more soda or something. Sorry, Ann. Getting involved this deep in your world is new to me."

"You sure fit in well, despite the strange circumstances," John remarked.

The steward opened the arena gate. "Okay gang, line up starting with sixth place and head out to line up by the red carpet."

We let everyone pass us, and Jennifer did not even look over at us as we followed behind her. I must say I felt a bit inhibited as we all paraded out the gate to where the show officials stood at the end of a rolled-out carpet by a table with ribbons, some envelopes, and a nice trophy topped with a horse and rider going over a jump.

One by one, the class winners rode up to accept ribbons and checks. Our turn was a little awkward for both us and the steward. I had no bridle to clip on the blue ribbon. Ann quietly said, "Use the harness."

The steward looked at me questioningly.

"It's fine. I don't bite," I said.

He smiled, laughed, and put it on me. Ann was given the envelope with her check and the trophy.

When we got back in line side by side as the spectators cheered next to us, Jennifer said just loud enough for us to hear, "Notice the trophy is not topped by a freak. It's a HORSE and rider. Not a centaur."

We all trotted around the arena on our victory lap, with us going first. I felt the same rush of joy that I felt when winning the state science fair. The whole arena erupted in cheering and camera flashes.

When we finished our circuit, we found Mom, Dad, Aunt Bonnie, Alice, Ben, and Mrs. Albert waiting outside by the exercise arena, surprisingly with the exchange student Robert Dickerson and his parents. All three of the Dickersons stared at us in wonder. I just smiled in a friendly manner, feeling more and more like a rare zoo animal.

"Remarkable," Mr. Dickerson said in his pleasant British accent. "Jerry, you could probably get into eventing all by yourself, if I may say so."

"Ann and I are a team, sir. I'm hoping for a career in Cosmology." My eyes dropped away for just a moment when I noticed a puddle near Robert's feet.

I was instantly hit with a vision in the water. There was a trim, thirty-ish man with a neat mustache dressed business casual in a tan sports coat. He was getting out of a golf cart parked near Mrs. Albert's van in the twilight. He was carrying an attaché case.

He put the case on the seat of the golf cart, opened it, took out what looked like a handgun, loaded it with a tranquilizer dart, and crept towards the van, keeping to the shadows. The vision vanished, leaving me with a horrible feeling of foreboding, accompanied with a bit of dizziness.

"Jerry, you, okay? You look pale, like you've seen a ghost," Mom began.

"In a way, I have." I let the words just slip out as I looked over at the Dickersons. "I have to leave now. Sorry, folks."

"Well, we'll see you another time. Great performance, you two," Mr. Dickerson said.

Robert came close. "Ann, I'll catch you on Facebook."

The Dickersons hurried off, talking excitedly to one another.

"What's wrong?" Ann touched my human shoulder.

"A vision. It's a centaur thing. I'm in danger. Serious danger. Someone is coming after me with a dart gun this evening at the van."

"Who?" Mom demanded sharply.

"I don't know. A man, thirty something with a mustache. It's a warning I'm not going to ignore. Let's talk more back at the van out of this crowd." I started to walk away from the arena towards Mike, surrounded by my family and friends.

Mike did a great job of keeping the crowds away from us. I remained as polite as I could be with all the well-wishers under the circumstances, smiling and waving as did Ann.

On the walk back to the van I considered foiling the obvious abduction plot by shifting back to my normal self and going home via the camper my parents had over in the park campground, but then what? I could easily be tracked down, and my family possibly put in danger.

I had no idea who this mystery man was, what organization he was connected to, or who called him in and all that was a major problem in trying to figure out any counter measures.

I began to consider after escaping home I should shift back to centaur, and run away to spend time with Chiron in that dimension until things blew over. But would they blow over?

Or would some unknown entity question my family, threaten torture, or worse and learn about the portal and try to break through? That would be a disaster of universal proportions.

I was pulled out of my thoughts by Ben barking, "Oh crap!"

Ann pulled back instinctively on the reins and Alice grabbed my breast strap to stop me.

I focused on two teams of media people with cameras and boom microphones waiting by the van. One was from WKYT and the other a RIDE-TV sports team. Mom and Dad rushed ahead while Aunt Bonnie, Mrs. Albert, Ben, and Alice formed a protective line with Mike on his horse between the media and Ann and me when they came closer to our approach.

"Just one minute," my dad burst out, holding out his hands.

"Stop right there a moment," Mike warned, reaching for his radio.

To keep from creating a scene, I said, "Dad, Mike, hold it. We'll answer a few questions. Let's keep it to three for me and three for Ann. I have to go on a cool out walk. Okay, guys?"

The media people all got the look of rabbits in the headlights. Mike kept his eyes on them.

"You talk?" the RIDE-TV sports newscaster exclaimed as he came a little closer with the others following tentatively.

"That's one down for me. Yes, I do. I have an IQ of 186, was in the gifted classes with my two friends here at Greenville High School, and was on the way to a career in Cosmology before this curse happened," I explained. "My sister's horse got injured, and can't compete the rest of the summer. I decided to make the best of my bad situation and help her. She wants to eventually get on the U.S. Equestrian Team and go into the Olympics."

The woman with the WKYT microphone came forward. "Rene Baker here, WKYT. This question is for your sister. Ann, whatever gave you the idea you could get your brother in his condition to stand in for your injured horse?"

"When I saw him jump the pasture fence after Gold Coast was injured. It took some convincing. But we're family no matter what. He's smarter and braver than anyone I know."

I wasn't expecting that, and I felt my face go hot.

"This is for Jerry," Ms. Baker continued. "I read you think it was a cursed stone or something that caused this. You believe magic is real, and do you think this curse can be reversed?"

"I'm living proof magic is real. The stone is the logical source, since the person holding it at the time called me a horse's ass before throwing the stone away. It was never recovered. I don't know how long this will last, but it has gone on for almost two months. Maybe it will end all on its own. Maybe not," I lied, but it was a needed and very convincing lie.

"Clay West, RIDE-TV here. This is for Ann. Ann, what are your show plans for the rest of the season?"

"Mr. West, I am working with my horse to help him recover. But meanwhile, my brother and I are a team. If we can make it to the other shows I've signed up to enter this season, we will. I don't want to mention locations for security reasons, but we seem to have been accepted among most of the other riders. Jerry and I have trained hard.

"This sport is new to him, and the jumps are as challenging to him as for any horse. Just because he's a genius centaur does not make it any less dangerous. If our timing or judgment is off, we can have an accident like any other horse and rider team."

"My last question is for Jerry," Ms. Baker quickly said. "Jerry, what will you do if this curse is permanent? You certainly will not be going to college in your condition, or fit into a research lab or observatory."

That really put me on the spot. I took my helmet off and rubbed my sweaty head. "I don't know . . . I really don't."

Mr. Braddock, from the back of a growing crowd, called, "You may be offered a job from the park or even the USEF for exhibition jumping. Anything can happen. Keep that door open, Jerry."

"We'll see. But thanks. It all depends on what happens with this curse," I answered.

"My last question for Ann," Mr. West interjected. "What are your plans for the future?"

"I'd like to join the US Equestrian team and go to the Olympics, like Jerry said. But I'd like to do it with Gold Coast. And if he is not healed, I'll have to train and use another horse. I'd say work with Jerry, but I hope the curse goes away so he can get into Cosmology and discover something new about the Universe. Though he may have already by proving magic is real and that it may be a part of physics we just have not discovered yet."

Her answer made me proud of her, and feel a little better about myself.

"You are both very wise for your age and should make your parents and community proud," Ms. Baker remarked.

The two media teams left to finish their sport commentary on the horse show, and we headed for the van with Mike, who stopped to talk to Mr. Braddock. Ann dismounted, and we all went together on a walk along the length of the Steeplechase Barn to cool me down in silence; internalizing what just happened with the media. Some people in the crowd and passing riders waved at us, while others did everything to ignore us as they passed by. The silence among us did not last long.

"Listen," I started, "as much as I don't like running out on Mrs. Albert and all, I really don't think I should stay here. It's too dangerous for me and all of you. I should go right home. Maybe I will make myself scarce for a while in the other dimension with Chiron. They will know everything that has happened with seers working all the time."

Mrs. Albert gave me a strange look. "I don't think you'll fit in the camper, and I have to be here for my classes that start at ten tomorrow."

I had totally forgotten we had not told Mrs. Albert about the ring. "Um-m-m," I stammered. "In all this drama of the show and all I forgot . . . we forgot to tell you I can change at will because of this ring. Long story. Can't go into it now. Sorry."

"Wow!" Mrs. Albert gasped. "What is important now is keeping you out of a lab or God only knows what. We all must face it square on and admit we knew something like this would happen. I'm not mad at you in the least."

"The only other choice we have is to catch the guy," Ben suggested hopefully.

"Ben, this is not one of our *D&D* adventures," Aunt Bonnie spoke up.

"Even with security's help, it would be far too dangerous," Mom said. "We just don't know who is involved."

"Your idea of shifting back and coming home with us and maybe staying with Chiron for a short time sounds like the most logical solution," Dad agreed.

"Use the van. With all that is going on here at the show, no one will notice a kid coming out of the van. And whoever that mystery man is, he will not find a centaur in the vehicle. Tonight, I can lock myself in and I do have an iPhone. Or I may just move to the show van and trailer parking area and find safety in the numbers of people over there," Mrs. Albert thought aloud.

"Are you sure you'll be, okay?" Dad asked.

"Sure." Mrs. Albert nodded. "Let's get you ready for the change, Jerry."

"Um-mm we have a problem. I have no clothes or shoes with me." I suddenly felt like an idiot.

"Can you fit in your sister's jeans? You already have a t-shirt on," Mom asked.

"I don't think so," I replied.

"Well, you may fit into one of my work jeans. I always pack extras just in case I get full of mud while working at the shows I go to. And I know my muck out rubber boots by Drama Queen's stall will fit you as they are a bit big on me," Mrs. Albert offered.

We headed back to the van. Mike was there, waiting. I knew we'd have to get him out of the way. "We have a minor problem," I whispered and nodded toward Mike.

My dad nodded and went over to him immediately. "Take a break. We'll be okay here now that the media is gone and Jerry will be in the van."

"Thanks, Mr. Swift," Mike said

. "Could use a break."

When Dad returned to us, he said, "The camper is in space 171, not far from this road. We'll be packed and ready to go by the time you walk there."

After hugs and goodbyes, Mom, Dad, Ann, Alice, and Ben headed for the campground while Aunt Bonnie and Mrs. Albert came with me into the van. They got my tack off and gave me a quick rub down.

Mrs. Albert brought a pair of jeans out of her dressing room and held them up so I could have a look. They appeared a bit wide, but that would not matter. This was an emergency and any pride would just have to take a back seat.

"I think they'll be just fine." I took them and the boots to the box stall I had been using.

I just put my hand on the stall door, ready to go in and start the shift, when I heard a golf cart drive up and froze where I stood. Aunt Bonnie and Mrs. Albert hurried from the van.

"Oh hi, Mr. Braddock," Mrs. Albert said loud and cheerily, meaning for me to hear her.

"Where are Ann and the rest of the family? I saw Jerry go in the van," Mr. Braddock asked.

"Family emergency," Aunt Bonnie replied, using her writer's imagination for a quick and logical answer. "Dad, Jerry's grandfather, had chest pains and was sent to the hospital. I'm on my way to get my truck to join them."

"I'm sorry to hear that. I wanted to talk to all of you about Ann and Jerry's future here and with USEF shows. But it can wait. I'll be in touch. I have their address, e-mail, and phone numbers."

I heard him get into the golf cart and drive off. I sighed deeply. That had been too close.

"All clear," Aunt Bonnie called. "We'll wait out here."

I stepped into the stall, stared at the ring, and whispered, "I wish to shift to my human form."

The pain hit. I blacked out and fell. I came to a bit disoriented, but it did not last. I quickly pulled on Mr. Albert's jeans and the muck-out boots, and staggered out of the stall to the top of the ramp to find them waiting at the bottom.

"You, okay?" Aunt Bonnie grabbed my arm to steady me as I was still a bit wobbly.

"A little dizzy, but fine," I answered. "Thanks for all your help in this, Mrs. Albert. I feel bad about deserting you."

She came over, hugged me, and whispered in my ear, "Don't. It was great what you did for your sister. You are a wonderful young man and have to watch out for yourself at this point. I hope everything works out, okay?" She followed it with a surprise kiss to my forehead.

The second she let go of me; Aunt Bonnie hugged me. "I'll see you at my place. Get going."

When she released me, I walked away from them, looking back only once to wave. Keeping an eye on the people I passed on the sidewalk to the Kentucky Horse Park Campground, I walked at a quick, but normal, pace. It was not far; maybe a couple hundred yards.

I found the camper easily at the very end of the outer loop, only yards from Nina Bonnie Boulevard and Campground Road. Everything was packed. We were not long in leaving the park grounds. No one spoke. I kept watching out the windows for any suspicious cars or trucks. Still, the forty-five-minute trip seemed like hours.

Dad pulled into Aunt Bonnie's drive and went to park right behind her house. The sun was just past its zenith. My watch read 2:05 p.m. In about ten minutes, she came up the drive in her truck with Alice and Ben. We all got out and gathered on her back porch. What should have been a great celebration was more like a funeral. Reality had closed in like black storm clouds.

"I'm not good at speeches," I began. "I only know that the scrying tells part of what is to happen. But what is seen is a warning and can be changed, and I hope we have done that for now. But the danger still remains. We don't know who the man is, or who he works for. I think it best I leave for a little while."

My peripheral vision caught movement by the shed. When I looked, everyone turned their heads. It was Chiron in the sun dappled shadows by the shed.

"Holy shi…." Ben started.

Chiron stepped into the light. I noticed he already had my bow, quiver of arrows, and the strap of my messenger bag in his right hand. He knew; had probably seen everything that happened at the show. He strode closer to the porch.

"I will take care of him. He has more schooling to do in my world," he said in his resonant voice.

My family, friends, and I hugged the group awkwardly.

Mom hung on the longest. Then she kissed both my cheeks. When she pulled back, there were tears in her eyes. “I’m so proud of you. Do what Chiron says. We’ll be all right.”

I nodded. When I looked beyond her, I could see both Alice and Ann had tears rolling down their cheeks. Ben was sniffing his tears back with an indifferent look on his face, and Aunt Bonnie was trying her best not to cry. Dad was stoic, as always.

I slowly backed away to follow Chiron toward the shed, feeling joy, sadness, and fear all roiling around in my gut like boiling liquid. I stepped to the side of the shed, out of sight of my family and friends.

Chiron stood quietly with his back to me as I took off the jeans and boots and shape shifted to centaur behind the shed. Thankfully, I did not black out for long.

I got to my feet and went around to the shed doors where Chiron was now waiting. I looked over to the house to find everyone still standing on the porch. They all waved. I waved back, fighting tears as I stared from one to the other as if to memorize each one in a mental photograph album.

Chiron handed me my bow, quiver of arrows, and messenger bag and I followed him into the shed with a deep knowing I would return.

THE END

THE JERRY SWIFT SERIES

Book 1
Jerry Swift and Chiron's Pride

Book 2
Jerry Swift and Herme's Revolt

Book 3
Jerry Swift and the Olympus War

All from Crossroads Publishing, LLC.

www.ingramcontent.com/pod-product-compliance
Lightning Source LLC
LaVergne TN
LVHW010648110826
845149LV00014B/2988

* 9 7 8 1 9 7 0 3 9 6 1 2 6 *